BEYOND THE LUNA

JOAQUIM SILVA

Dear Danielle,
I hope this book inspires
you to follow your dreams!

Silva

ISBN: 978-0-9576401-0-8

Joaquim Silva prefers paper-free publishing wherever possible.

Dear Danielle,
I hope this book inspires
you to follow your dreams!

Silva

Author's Note

This is a tale that will be forged by your hand as you turn each page, and as the young boy in this story dreams, discovers, and learns to love the adventure of life...

I hope the same happens for you.

To anyone who looks up to the stars and dreams...

BEYOND THE LUNA

CHAPTER ONE

The Fallen Hero

"A dreamer is one who can find his way by moonlight"

- Oscar Wilde

Beauty needs a witness, and it was reflected in his brown eyes as he waited for the stars to appear. A cold wind that promised winter tore through the creamy sky, and slowly aided the ship's voyage along the Atlantic Ocean. On the deck, a boy leaned over the railing and watched as the dark waves crashed into the boat's hull. The sky soon turned black, and the night breeze ruffled his dark wavy hair. Wearing only a T-shirt and jeans was proving a bit chilly, but the night sky was breathtaking. As the full moon crept out from behind the clouds, it gently lit his soft olive skin. It was his first and last night on the boat and he wanted to make the most of it. I wish I could stay here forever, the boy thought, but he knew summer was almost over and he would soon be going back to school. He perished the thought returning to academia and being forced to study subjects he disliked. Looking up at the stars helped him forget. What he really wanted was to learn about the moon, the stars, and maybe even become an astronaut. But he knew this quixotic dream of his would be frowned upon by his parents, even his teachers and school friends would laugh whenever he expressed his love for astronomy. The vast majority of the other kids at school had a somewhat penchant to dismiss childlike dreams, opting for a more serious future in business or law. His parents had pushed him down the path of studying math, something he really loathed and had no passion in. Often in classes he would stare out the window, which would always result in him being shouted at, but his teachers would never understand that he was just curious and dreaming. His parents had gone on their annual summer trip to the Azores Islands, and they had also enrolled him in summer school - because his math grades were slacking. Deep down he just wanted to tell them about his dreams and inclinations of studying the stars, but he knew if the situation did come to pass, the small voice in his head would stop him from speaking his truth. The sudden sound of shouting snapped him out of the moonlight's trance.

'Luis! Luis where are you?'

He recognized his mother's voice calling him.

Luis looked to his right, and heard the ominous sound of heeled shoes tapping on the hardwood deck. His mom walked up beside him. She fastened the buttons on her cardigan, and crossed her arms to defend the cold blustery air.

'What are you doing out here all by yourself?'

Luis opened his mouth to answer, but she cut him off. 'And with no jacket, do you want to catch a chill!?'

Luis watched as her brown hair danced in the wind.

'Your father will be really annoyed if he sees you out here, you're supposed to be in your room studying.'

Luis exhaled and slumped his shoulders. She put her warm hand on his straight nose, now slightly shiny with grease, and lightly pinched it.

'Come on let's go!'

Luis watched her walk away. With each step, the sound of her shoes grew fainter. He looked at the moon one last time and closed his eyes.

'Give me the courage to follow my dreams,' he whispered.

His mother called for him once more, and he opened his eyes and looked to the moon, but it was gone - shrouded behind the dark clouds.

The ship was an incredible spectacle, over fifty feet long with spiraling staircases that led to the upper decks. He took his time catching up, and peering in some of the windows, he spotted what looked like a small ballroom, and a casino. A raised section of the deck contained more outdoor amenities, such as a small gym and a grand outdoor swimming pool. Walking past he noticed the stars in the night sky glistening on the water's reflection. It had such aesthetic appeal, but his mom never noticed. He followed her through a door, down a flight of stairs, and into the ship's hold. A soft beige carpet cushioned his feet as he lumbered through the corridor, and his mom shuddered with the transition from cold to warm.

'I don't know how you managed to stay outside for so long without a jacket.'

Luis too busy admiring the size of the ship's decor ignored her. The hallway of doors looked like it stretched on for miles, and as they walked through, Luis noticed next to every door, was a small boat themed abstract art picture - encapsulated in a square mahogany frame. Small wrinkles appeared on his forehead as he looked around.

'Where is everyone?' Luis asked.

'Well the majority of passengers departed at Porto and everyone else must be sleeping, because we arrive in port Lisbon soon.'

She reached into her cardigan pocket and pulled out what looked like a plastic credit card, she inserted it in the door and turned around.

'Now make sure you remember the door number, 295.'

Luis rolled his eyes, nodded his head, and followed his mom into the room. She quietly closed the door behind her and whispered to him.

'Hurry on in to the next room, and start your math work before your father sees you.'

Luis didn't want to get in any more trouble, so he complied straight away . He walked into his small room on the ship and turned the light on, but unfortunately his father was already in the room.

'Where have you been!?' his father scathed.

Luis looked up at him shocked.

'I was outside on the deck.'

'Staring into space again I'm guessing?'

'No I was taking a break.'

'Taking a break...for an hour and a half?'

Luis didn't respond and just stared at the floor, and his father walked out of the room. He sighed and heard his father speaking with his mom.

'One hour and thirty minutes he spent out there.'

'You know how he is...he loves looking out at the night sky.'

'Stop pampering him. If he carries on, he'll be looking out at the night sky everyday from the streets...because he won't have a well-paid job.'

Luis sat down on the nearby chair, rested his head on the table and clenched his teeth. He hated when his family denounced his dreams in front of him.

He covered his ears with his arms, but his father marched back into the room and called his name. Luis looked up at him slowly, his father's face was contorted, and his eyebrows were frowned.

'Look Luis, I know it sounds like I'm angry with you, but I'm not. I'm just frustrated because I've worked so hard to provide for you and your mom, and I don't want to see you fail.'

'But I don't like Maths, and you keep forcing me to take extra classes.'

'So what do you like then?' his father asked.

Luis knew any answer would be the wrong answer, but he went for it anyway.

'I want to study space, like the moon and the stars, maybe even become an astronaut.'

Luis's father closed his eyes, and for a second Luis thought his words had finally sunk in. But then, his father shook his head in disapproval.

'Just because you like staring into space, doesn't mean you can make a career out of it. You're growing up now, and I'm not going to sugar coat things for you like your mother. But this dream you have of becoming an astronaut is stupid!'

Luis looked up at him sadly.

'Look, we all had dreams like you when we were young, I wanted to be a footballer, but by the time I reached your age I realized it wasn't going to happen.'

'Yeah but I really want this.'

'I know you do, but soon you'll realize you have to opt for something more realistic in life. That's why, we've enrolled you in these extra math classes.'

'But it's not want I want to do,' argued Luis.

'Yes but we know what's best for you! And right now this astronaut vocation of yours is rather...how can I put it in a word you might understand...alien.'

Luis knew in his heart he wasn't going to win this argument, so he gave up. His father had hurt him, and he just wanted some time alone.

'Okay...I have work to do, so I need to concentrate,' said Luis and he gestured to the door.

'I'll be checking it tomorrow, so don't stay up too late. Goodnight.'

His father smiled and went into the next room. As straight as he was gone, Luis got up and shut the door. That horrible lump had formed in his throat, and with his T-shirt, he dabbed away the water that was building around his eyes. There was a math textbook on the table, Luis sat down, opened a random page, and lethargically started reading.

*

Hours had passed and Luis could hear his dad snoring in the opposite room. He was glad his parents had fallen asleep, having gotten bored of his father denigrating him for his persistent daydreaming. Normally at home he would just go into his room and shut the door, but being on the boat made things more difficult. Back in Lisbon his father was a doctor, a job which contained many hours of study, intertwined with unwavering hours of focus. This was the main reason his dad was always so strict with him, in terms of being focused and committed. However, Luis found it challenging to become good at a subject he disliked, he could put up with frequent lessons at school, but doing extra work felt like a chore. Luis shut the book, he hadn't finished his work, but he was growing tired and his mind was wavering. He wondered what his life would be like, if he followed his father's footsteps and became a doctor. But he couldn't forge an image in his mind. He yawned, and laid down on the bed and tried to fall asleep, but found himself reminiscing about past times. He thought about his recent school year, and how the majority of kids always looked at him as being the cosseted "only child." But deep down he knew things were quite the contrary. He continued to think about school, and slowly conjuring up inside him, was that dire feeling of returning. It was the same feeling he would get every Sunday night, when he would pack his bag and he knew he was looking down the barrel of a long arduous week. But it was those thoughts that triggered in him, the sensation of following something he loved. Luis was fortunate enough to have a skylight in his room on the boat. He looked up at the stars and remembered his first glimpse of staring into the night sky. He had received a telescope from his uncle, on one of his birthdays, and every day he would rush home from school, grab a yoghurt and a banana from the fridge, play football till it was dark, then come inside and spend hours looking at the constellations. He knew his love for astronomy wasn't superficial, because no family or friends had persuaded him into it. His connection that he had formed with the stars was visceral. Time passed and Luis tossed and turned in his bed. It was incredibly silent, and he could hear the clock ticking. He turned around and read the time - 9:00pm. Yawning he put his hands under the cold pillow, and stuck one of his legs out of the cover. He felt his eyes grow heavy, and just like the boat drifting at sea, he slowly drifted to sleep.

*

Some time passed and underneath his eyelids he felt a powerful, illuminating light pierce his sound sleep. He opened his eyes in the darkness, but the intensity was overwhelming. He drew his hands out from under the pillow and rubbed his eyes, and they slowly adjusted to the brightness. He looked up and realized the light was streaming down from the skylight above. He got out of bed and looked at the clock, the time read 11:30pm.

Slipping on his trousers, he peered into the next room and checked on his parents who were still fast asleep. He went back into his room, leapt on the bed and stood under the light.

'What is that?' he said silently.

Now filled with curiosity, he jumped off the bed and put on his shoes. Creeping into his parent's room he snatched the room key and tiptoed to the door. He put his palm on the handle and with one swift move opened the door and slid out into the hallway. He walked down the hall and climbed the steps to the upper deck, it was cold and goose bumps appeared on his forearms as he walked out. Luis looked everywhere, but no one was around. He turned to his left and seen another staircase twisting up toward the main deck, he walked up and realized it was just as deserted. Frustrated he looked up to the sky, but he couldn't see the moon. He thought of exploring the ship, but shrugged off his curiosity, and decided to give up finding the mysterious source of light.

'Maybe it was just a dream,' he said as he walked back down. The cold night air hit his body, and he scurried into the hallway, to get back in his warm bed. He stopped outside door number 325 and inserted the room key, he pushed the handle, but nothing happened. He tried once more, this time exerting more force, and barging the door with his shoulder, but to no avail. Panic rapidly spread throughout his face. How could I have forgotten the door, he thought! He tried a multitude of doors but none of them worked. He knew if he knocked on them, and his parent's caught him, he'd be in so much trouble. Breathing heavily, he stood outside door number 395. Holding his breath and hoping, he put the key card in the door, and pulled it out with one quick swipe...but nothing happened. He slid down the door, and collapsed onto the carpet. A lump formed in his throat, and a small teardrop ran down his face. He smudged the droplet around his cheek and sat there staring at the wall. Suddenly a cold wind hit his face, Luis looked around, and saw a door held ajar by the wind. He walked over and followed it outside to the main deck. A small flickering light in the distance sparked his curiosity, and he ventured further. The sound of the ocean waves were extremely loud on this side of the ship, and he carried on walking forward, until he reached a dead end. There was a small ladder in front of him, and with nothing to lose he climbed up to the top. What he saw took his breath away. Luis realized he was now standing on the ship's bow. In front of him was the biggest full moon he had ever seen. Hypnotized by its beauty, he continued walking forward.

'Wow, this is amazing!' he exclaimed.

Something caught his eye, and he unconsciously climbed over the railing to get a better look. He knew, one step wrong could prove fatal, but he walked up the acute apex of the bow. Slowly he reached the very edge, and with his eyes shut, walked into the moonlight's narrow beam. The chilly wind snapped him back to reality, and opening his eyes he suddenly realized what he was doing. He peered down thirty feet below, and watched the black sea water being powerfully pushed by the concentrated power of the boat. Sensing the proximity of danger, he turned around and started to retreat. The ship was traveling at an immense speed, and suddenly it hit something submerged under the surface. The velocity of the impact knocked the boat off its equilibrium, and the blunt force threw Luis into the air. He let out a huge scream of terror as he crashed into the icy water below. He resurfaced and screamed for his life, but no one could hear him, and he watched as the ship sailed away into the night. All of a sudden a wave smacked him hard, the cold salty sea water filled his lungs, and choked him, restricting any more cries for help. Another huge wave crashed into him from his left side and dragged him under the water.

His lungs craved for air but he couldn't find a leverage

to pull up to the surface. Water pushed down on him from all sides, and dragged him deep under. The moonlight on the water's surface now seemed miles away. He had no more fight left in him. Luis submitted to the darkness, and let the water take him.

CHAPTER TWO

Journey To The Moon and Back

"I'm not the same having seen the moon shine on the other side of the world"

- Mary Hershey

On a distant Island, a young girl named Marina sat on a wooden walkway overlooking the ocean. An impression of insignificance radiated from her body language, as she dangled her feet over the edge, and watched the still sea. There was no wind at all, and her long black hair camouflaged well with the pitch black sky. She stood up, whispered something to herself, and pulled out a necklace from her undergarment. Her lips slightly rouged, kissed the pendant. She turned her attention to the sky, and her rich hazel eyes, framed in long lashes, drank in the darkness. Marina turned around and walked down the narrow boardwalk, it was quiet and her footsteps echoed in the night air. She reached the end and walked along the cinnamon coloured sandy beach, but suddenly she heard a noise emit near the rocks. She looked over her shoulder to investigate, and in shock horror spotted a small dark figure washed up on the surface. She squinted her eyes for a moment, then ran home as quick as she could. Outside her house she spotted her brother cleaning his small boat with a cloth.

'Raul, you have to help me! I think someone has washed up on the shore!'

Raul looked shocked. He had never seen his sister in such a state of panic. Marina ran back to the beach frantically.

'Hurry!'

Raul ran after her, leaving a trail of sand-dust behind him. He spotted the boy lying lifeless on the sand, and quickly flipped him over. With his two hands, he pressed down hard on the boy's chest.

'Is anything happening!?' yelled Marina, her eyes darting in concern as she spoke. Raul didn't respond, he breathed into the boy's mouth and repeated compressing his chest. He breathed into his mouth once more, this time the boys chest rose! Raul pushed his chest again, and suddenly the boy coughed out the salty sea water, that was trapped in his lungs. The young boy opened his bloodshot eyes. Raul tilted the boy up and lightly tapped him on the back, and he coughed out more water.

'Is he gonna be okay!?' asked Marina.

Raul gave his sister a reassuring look, and turned to the boy who was slowly coming to his senses.

'What's your name?' asked Raul.

With his right hand, Raul brushed off the speckles of sand from the boy's mouth.

'Do you have a name?' Raul asked once more.

'Luis, my name's...Luis,' he whispered before shutting his eyes.

'We have to get him inside, somewhere warm. Go back to the house, and tell dad what happened, tell him to light the fireplace,' said Raul.

Marina dashed to the house, whilst Raul picked Luis up. He whispered to him, hoping he could hear his voice 'You're gonna be okay kid.'

*

Luis woke up some hours later. Slowly opening his eyes he realized he was no longer on the beach. The smell of the sea was replaced by the sound of a burning fire, and he felt an intense warm heat from behind him. He turned around, and watched the orange and red embers, flicker above the flames. Luis felt his clothes - they were still slightly wet, shivering he wrapped his arms round his chest, and curled up to keep warm. Raul peering in from the kitchen noticed Luis had woken up, he walked into the room, and stood near the fire.

'How you feeling?'

Luis looked at him, his teeth were chattering, too cold to speak he just nodded at Raul.

'Look I'm gonna be in the kitchen, my mom is making some warm soup for you, if there's anything you need just let me know okay?'

Raul started to walk to the kitchen but before he exited, Luis turned around to face him.

'Hey, thank you...for saving me.'

Raul flashed a small smile.

'Anytime.'

Luis noticed Raul was as tall as the door frame. He had a very athletic build, with a chiseled look. He carried with him an air of uncertainty, a sort of calming, enigmatic presence. Luis put one hand on the nearby chair and pulled himself up. He walked round the small room, it looked like the inside of a somewhat renovated ram-shackle cabin. The floor was wooden, but there was a huge circular rug that gave the room a real cosy feel. Above the fireplace was a homemade mantelpiece, atop it were ornaments that resembled fishes and sea creatures. In the middle there was a small golden trophy, in the shape of a fishing rod. Luis's picked it up and read the description.

*"Presented by His Majesty King Jorge
as a perpetual trophy for outstanding Fisherman"*

'I didn't know you liked fishes that much, maybe we should have left you in the water.'

Raul's voice rattled Luis, and he nearly dropped the trophy.

'Easy now, my dad will kill ya if you damaged his pride and joy...or worse kill me for saving your life!'

Raul laughed and Luis put the trophy back.

'I'm only messing with you kid...here, your soup's ready, this will warm you right up.'

Raul handed Luis the soup in a warm flask, and watched him drink it.

'What'd I tell ya?' Luis took one more gulp and thanked Raul once more. Raul flicked his hair over his face and scratched the small stubble under his chin.

'How old are you?' asked Luis.

'Seventeen,' said Raul.

Before Luis could comment, Marina walked into the room, she looked at her brother sternly.

'Hey you never told me he was awake.'

'I wanted to get him settled in,' responded Raul.

Marina walked toward the open fire and shook Luis's hand.

'My name's Marina. I was the one who spotted you on the shore.'

Luis looked at her, and noticed she was wearing a gold necklace, its centerpiece tucked under her shirt.

Raul extended his right hand and gave Luis a firm handshake.

'Since I haven't formally introduced myself I might as well do it now, I'm Raul.'

Luis continued to drink his soup.

'Let me know if you need anymore,' said Marina as she watched him drink it down.

'I'm fine, but thank you,' responded Luis.

Luis put the flask down on the floor, and stood up.

'Thank you, both of you, but I really need...'

Before he could finish his sentence he started to feel faint again. Raul leapt out of his seat and guided Luis back down safely in his chair.

'You need to take it easy,' Luis rested his back in the chair and noticed, standing in the hall was a woman.

'Don't worry, that's just my mom,' said Marina.

She introduced her to Luis, and he shook her hand. She was a petite woman, slightly smaller than his own mother, her hair was tied into a neat and precise bun, and not a single strand was out of place.

'Thank you for the soup,' said Luis.

She smiled at him, but before she could speak, a gruff voice from the other side of the room interjected.

'No need to thank her, you should be thanking me!'

Luis turned around and saw a large beefy, muscular

man, his hands covered in charcoal, and carrying logs of wood.

'I'm the one who bought her the ingredients,' he said, winking at his wife.

Marina's mom looked at Luis embarrassed.

'And that man right there is my husband, and if you've already met my son, you can see where he gets his cheekiness from.'

Marina's father marched over and shook Luis's hand.

'So I hear your name's Luis?'

'Yes.'

Marina's father put his hand on Luis's head and ruffled his damp hair.

'Raul you're meant to be a fisherman like me! That means catching fish, not little boys.'

Marina's mother intervened.

'Always with the jokes, you know sometimes it's hard to tell when you're being serious. If it wasn't for Marina and Raul... he might not have survived.'

She gave Luis a reassuring look.

'Relax, he knows I'm joking! Raul, you did good, I'm really proud of you.'

He took his hand off Luis's head and threw some wood down on the fire. Luis watched as their mother and father exchanged brief witty insults toward one another. Marina couldn't take her eyes off Luis, something was intriguing her.

'So what Island are you from?' she asked.

Luis looked at her extremely confused.

'What do you mean, Island?'

'Which…Island are you from?'

'I'm not sure, I'm not from around here,' replied Luis.

Marina's mother patted her on the shoulder.

'Let him rest Marina, he's been through an awful lot.'

As her mother walked back to the kitchen, Luis spoke.

'I need to get back home, do you know any where I can get on a boat?'

Marina's mother stood dead in her tracks, and very subtly the atmosphere in the room dived. Her mother turned around, and not looking directly at him responded.

'I don't think that's possible dear, it's very late, I don't think there are any boats available.'

Luis looked at Marina, who seemed strangely worried. Sensing his wife was having trouble, Marina's father spoke up.

'Err what my wife means is…it's just not possible at this time.'

'But I don't understand, where I'm, from boats travel all the time, I really need to get back home! My mom and dad are going to be worried!' said Luis quickly.

Raul noticing the awkward situation cut in.

'Luis I think right now the best thing for you is to get some rest.'

Luis became irritated, he got up and walked to the door. Marina yelled at him to come back, but the vibe in the room had changed, and he wanted to return home.

'You don't understand I need to go home, thanks for looking after me, but I really have to go!'

He waved goodbye and walked out the door. Marina's mother tried to go after him, but her husband blocked her with his arm.

'Maybe he's just got slight amnesia from the accident. Let him go. He'll find out sooner or later.'

Marina's mother turned to Raul.

'Keep an eye on him.'

Luis roamed to the end of the boardwalk. There were wooden barriers on the sides, and the end of the boardwalk - three small wooden poles, that could be easily walked round. At first he thought it was quite dangerous, but then he remembered the fishermen, and divers. He tried to look toward the horizon, but his view was tainted by a ghastly shadow. He had been on the beaches in the night back home, but it was nothing like this. Something just felt wrong, Luis looked up at the sky and a huge unpleasant feeling entrenched his body. The sky was pitch black, no clouds, no stars. Luis looked around and spotted the moon. His jaw dropped and he went numb with fright. A small yellow crescent moon, with huge black cracks in its body, vaguely shone in the sky. It was like the moon was breaking apart. Luis, now really scared, began retreating down the boardwalk, until he bumped into something. He turned around, and spotted Raul. Luis flashed him a scared look and continued tracking back. Raul with his hands behind his back walked up toward him slowly.

'Luis, what's wrong?'

Stuttering frantically Luis responded.

'Wh-what is this place! Where am I?'

Luis looked at Raul untrustingly, motioning with his eyes he looked toward Raul's hands. Raul knew what he was trying to communicate, and took his hands from his back, and held them in the air - palms facing Luis to show he wasn't hiding anything. Luis gasping for his breath stopped retreating.

'I'm sorry... I just want to go home,' he muttered.

Luis looked down at the wooden planks of the boardwalk, and in between the small horizontal gaps he could see the ocean not moving and realized it was more like a lake. Pulling in his focus, he noticed his shadow on the boardwalk floor. Then he saw something extremely haunting. Instantly he pushed Raul away and started retreating again.

'Luis, now what's wrong?' asked Raul.

Luis pointed his index finger at him aggressively.

'Stay the hell away from me! I don't know who you

are... but move back now!'

Raul put his hands in the air again.

'Luis seriously?'

'I said, stay away from me.'

Luis was almost at the end of the boardwalk, and Raul slowly kept advancing forward.

'Luis what's the matter? You have to tell me?'

'You haven't got a shadow,' Luis stuttered. 'Where's your shadow?'

Luis pointed out his own shadow under the dim light near boardwalk.

'You can see mine...what or who are you!?' snarled Luis. He picked up a small rock lying near the wooden pole and held it up like a weapon. Raul took a step forward to try and disarm him, but Luis swung at him! Suddenly someone let out a huge high pitched scream nearby.

'Luis. No!'

Luis inches away from Raul's temple bone, spotted Marina and halted his movement. In an instant - Raul disarmed Luis and threw the rock into the water. Marina walked closer, she knew in her heart Luis wouldn't hurt her. As she reached him, Luis looked down, and noticed Marina didn't have a shadow either.

'Luis you have to let us explain, it's finally dawned on me...'

'What has?' asked Luis.

'You're not from this world are you?'

Luis stayed silent, he was still confused.

'You don't know what Island you're from
because...you don't live here.'

Marina looked at his shadow.

'You can't be from around here. Everyone from here,
has had their shadow taken.'

Luis furrowed his brow, and looked at her really
confused. She walked past him, and moved right to the
edge of the boardwalk and gazed at the horizon.

'You're probably wondering where you are?'

Luis nodded slowly.

'I want you to listen to me Luis. Really listen to what
I'm about to tell you. Open your heart, your mind, and
really concentrate on my voice.'

Luis looked on curiously.

'This is Adastra...a parallel world that connects to
yours, through the sea and the night sky. I apologize to
you on behalf of my parent's behavior, but they were
only trying to be comforting. You see, at the moment
our land isn't in the greatest of states. Years ago Adastra
was once a beautiful place. The sea that we're standing
above used to shine a elegant emerald green, and the
sky above us used to be filled with a myriad of
stars...and the moon the delicate deity of our land, used
to bestow us with its radiant, illuminating light...but

now the stars no longer twinkle, and the moon doesn't shine. Adastra consists of four Islands, all surrounded by the Sea of Serenity. The land was once ruled over by a great King, who looked after Adastra, and inspired all of its creatures and inhabitants. But some time ago he fell upon a mysterious fate. Then by some malevolent force, a dark shadow poured through the province. It encapsulated the stars, drove the land into despair, and slowly it eclipsed, and seeped into the moon, stealing its lunar luminescence. Soon the shadow that is looming over the horizon, will be thrown over us like a curtain of darkness...if something isn't done quickly, Adastra will succumb to this veil of haze. All we have now is hope...hope that soon this nebulous of evil will pass, and the moonlight will shine bright once more.'

Her heartfelt message struck Luis profoundly, and he finally understood the situation. He turned to face the ocean with her, and together the three of them overlooked the Sea of Serenity.

'Every night I would come out here to this exact spot, and make a wish to the moon, that one day someone would come and save Adastra...I think that person is you Luis,' said Marina.

Slowly it dawned on him, and he started to remember his words on the ship. He walked to the edge of the boardwalk, and stood there in silence.

'What's wrong?' asked Marina.

'Before I landed here...I was on a ship with my parents, and I made a wish to the moon asking for courage... and then by accident I fell off the ship, and got transported here.'

'See, this is fate, you're going to help save Adastra from the darkness,' said Marina.

'Save Adastra, what do you mean?'

'Me and Raul have been saying for months now that we want to visit the King, and get to the bottom of this weird mystery. Now you can come with us!'

'Wait! I never said yes to anything,' responded Luis - deep down he was frightened, of what might happen to him if he pursued this wild adventure. He shrugged off his curiosity and shook his head.

'Sorry, I can't.'

Raul having gleaned his idiosyncrasies confronted him.

'You say you want courage, you wish for it longingly! But when the opportunity arises you don't take it. Courage doesn't come before the adventure Luis, courage will come to you when you act despite your fears.'

Raul pointed to the beach.

'When I saw you lying lifeless on the sand over there, I was scared, but I acted anyway, and now you're alive. I take my chances, and life rewards me, and in this case the others around me as well.'

Marina grabbed Luis's hand.

'I know you're scared, and you want to go home, but the only way back is by boat, and right now without the moon controlling the tides, you can't go anywhere.'

Luis looked out toward the Sea of Serenity, he realized no moon, meant no tide.

'I guess I have no choice...I'll do it,' said Luis, with a faint confidence in his voice.

Marina smiled and moved in to hug Luis, but his trailing foot slipped off the edge of the boardwalk, Luis fell! Marina let out a small scream, and quickly extended out her right arm. Luis by the skin of his teeth grabbed on.

'Raul I need your help!' she screamed.

Raul leapt up and held onto her legs. Marina dangling over the edge, looked at Luis's scared eyes.

'Don't worry I've got you.'

Raul grasped his hand over his sister's and together they pulled Luis up. But Marina's pendant under her shirt suddenly broke off.

'My necklace!'

But Luis grabbed it with his right hand in mid-flight.

With one final exertion they lifted Luis up to safety. He wiped the dust off his shirt and thanked the pair for saving him once again.

'Thank you for saving my necklace,' said Marina.

Luis about to give it back to her, examined it under the

dim light. It was a small golden crescent moon dangling down from a shiny gold chain.

'Wow, it's amazing,' said Luis. 'Mind if I try it on?'

'Go ahead.'

Luis threw the chain over his head and then... something incredible happened. A thundering sound broke over the sky, and huge gusts of wind flowed through the land. Marina's hair blew gracefully in the new wind, and a loud hissing sound filled the air. Underneath them the ground rumbled, and shook the boardwalk. All of them held on to each other for dear life.

'Look! Look at the sea!' yelled Raul.

The once still ocean began to move, and it gently started to crash against the rocks. Raul kept trying to get their attention, but something else had caught Marina's and Luis's eyes. Up in the sky there was a dim glow from the moon, and to their delight some of the black inky cracks had vanished.

'What on earth just happened?' said Raul excitingly.

Marina looked at her pendant, which was dangling from Luis's neck.

'It must have been when Luis put on the chain.'

Luis looked at her and started to believe in what he'd just witnessed.

'You never told me your pendant had some special power!' said Luis.

'I never knew,' replied Marina.

They all stared at the sea and the moon, until Raul spoke.

'We have to go! With the tide working now, we don't know how much time we have. We have to sail to Keplar Castle, and find out what's going on.'

'Keplar Castle?' Luis wondered.

*

Raul stopped them before they walked through the front door of the house.

'Now look, we can't tell anyone what we've just witnessed. If we're not careful our parents will pass their caution on to us, and stop us from going, and we can't let that happen.'

They all agreed.

'It will take a couple of hours to reach the castle, so we should take some supplies for the boat,' said Raul.

'Luis we haven't got much time, go into the kitchen and pour some of our mom's soup, into three separate flasks - you can find them in the cupboard under the sink.'

'Okay.'

'As soon as you're done meet me in my room,' said Marina.

Raul opened the door slowly, and the three of them

entered the house.

'Marina, pack a few things, and meet me on the beach in ten minutes,' he whispered.

Marina's mother and father had both fallen asleep in the chair near the fireplace. She crept to her room, and Luis went into the kitchen. He spotted a huge pot simmering on a low fire, and he poured the soup into the three flasks evenly. A delightful aroma of spices filled the air, as he closed each flask lid tight. He joined Marina in her room and she put the flasks in her backpack. Luis noticed her bedroom window looked out toward the sea.

'Wow what a great view,' he expressed.

Marina, packing her bag and brushing her hair simultaneously, responded.

'I remember when I used to stare out toward the ocean every night, it was almost like sea breeze had secrets to tell me.'

Luis looked at her longingly - he knew exactly what she meant. Marina opened her draw and pulled out a large folded piece of paper.

'This will come in handy!'

'What is that?' asked Luis.

'This is a map of Adastra - it will show us how to get to the King's castle.'

She opened the window and a humid breeze slipped through the room.

'Come on, let's go, we have to meet Raul,' said Marina as she jumped out the window.

Luis followed her and together they walked through the beach. There was a huge trail in the sand leading to the ocean, as Raul had already dragged the boat out. Luis and Marina joined him by the sea. But Marina gave Raul a worried look.

'What's wrong?' asked Raul.

'I feel bad, just leaving mom and dad, and not saying anything.'

'It's for the greater good Marina, you know that,' said Raul sharply.

Luis helped Marina load the boat - which conveniently was just enough to fit three people. Raul attached the sail and told the others to get in. Luis hopped in and sat next to Marina.

'I'm going to push the boat into the water. When I do, Luis I'm gonna need you to raise the sail,' said Raul.

Raul knelt down and slowly pushed the boat into the water, but a loud voice echoed through the air giving them all a fright.

'An just where do you think you're going!' Yelled Marina's father.

Raul instantly stood up straight and stopped what he was doing. Marina yelled from the back of the boat.

'Dad we're sorry…we didn't tell you it's just...'

Her father cut in quickly.

'All of you, get out now!' he snapped.

Marina and Luis stepped out of the boat and they all stood in front of him. He looked at his son.

'Raul you're not going anywhere...not without this.'

Behind his back he produced a long blue cape, made of rich fabric. It was stitched seamlessly, and on its underside there was a small logo of a moon and a star. He handed it to Raul.

'Wow what is it?' pondered Raul.

'That cape has something to do with the Royal Family of Adastra, but I'm not sure of its purpose. Your uncle and I, found it fishing one day.'

Raul fastened it round his neck and it fell loosely from his shoulders.

'If you're going to find out what happened to the King, you'd better take it with you. The royal insignia is embroidered underside, so it must have some significance,' said Marina's father.

Marina looked at him curiously.

'Dad, how did you know we were going?'

'I knew something strange had happened when I felt the wind blow through what's left of my hair! I went to your room, and for the first time in a while I could hear the ocean. Then I came out here and saw the moon.'

'I think it has something to do with the chain you gave me dad,' said Marina.

Marina's father stared at Luis who was wearing it.

'That's no ordinary chain Marina, it's a powerful medal that was given to me by the King.'

He saw Luis looking at him curiously.

'I used to be a fisherman for the prestigious royal family of Adastra, I was very good friends with the King, and he gave me that pendant as a gift for Marina's thirteenth birthday.'

Marina's father remembering the King looked down at the ground and sighed.

'Do you know what can explain all the mysterious goings on? asked Luis.

'The only thing I remember is, one day me and their uncle went to visit the King in his castle, but we weren't allowed in for some strange reason. Soon after, we were told the King had gone missing. Then from nowhere a strange dark cloud started emanating from his castle, and started swallowing the land.'

'What about your uncle, does he know anything?' asked Luis.

'You know, that's a good question,' he turned to Marina and Raul.

'Before you head off to the castle, go visit your uncle, I haven't spoken to him in months due to the tide not working. Maybe he can shed some light on this whole situation.'

'That's a great idea!' said Raul.

'One last thing before you go.'

He buried his hand deep in his pocket, pulled out a small compass, and threw it to Luis.

'You'll need this for when you're out at sea!'

Luis caught it and smiled back.

'Well you better hurry because that weird shadow is looming ever closer.'

'Thanks dad,' said Marina.

'I'm not gonna tell your mother either. Say hi to your uncle from me! Now go on hurry!'

Raul pushed the boat out into the water, and Luis raised the sail. The fresh wind blasted the huge white cloth, and powerfully pushed the boat out to sea. They waved goodbye, and the trio sailed out to save Adastra.

CHAPTER THREE

Sailing Into Uncharted Waters

"I have loved the stars too fondly to be fearful of the
 night"

- Galileo Galilei

Miles away from Oasis Island, the small boat swayed
along the ocean. Luis breathed in the air, and glanced
over his shoulder. Ironically the Sea of Serenity was
dark and somber, almost like it was guarding a secret
beneath its murky waters.
'How much further Raul?' asked Marina.
Raul, controlling the ship's rudder changed direction.
'We should arrive on Aquatic Reef Island in around
twenty minutes.'
Luis looked at Marina who was drinking some of her
soup.
'So have you been to this Island before?'
'We used to go all the time, to visit our uncle. It's a
really beautiful isle filled with lovely nature, but I can't

bear to think what it might look like now.'

'What about your Island, are you the only people that reside there?'

'Oasis Island? No there are many other families, but no one comes out anymore. Everyone is just afraid of the darkness,' she said in a depressed tone.

'Don't sound so defeated Marina! That's why we're here, to find out! We're explorers now guys, and you can't find anything new, if you're unwilling to leave the shore,' said Raul energetically.

*

The boat pulled up near the rocky shore. The beach was made out of pebbles, and there was a substantial amount of raised rocks near the surface. Luis and Marina followed Raul hopping from rock to rock.

'I'm guessing this is how the Island got its name?' said Luis.

'You bet, this isle is full of rocky reefs!' said Marina.

They landed on a zigzagging trail made of pebbles, and as they were walking, Luis stopped to look at the thick shadow, that seemed to be edging closer to the Island.

'Come on, we have to hurry,' warned Raul.

Luis caught up, and together they dashed up the hill. Reaching the top, Marina and Raul were shocked at how barren the Island had become. Huge dangling palm trees encompassed the area, and a few cabin like houses were scattered around. Their uncle's house was in the cabin furthest down, in front of a towering forestation. The trio walked up the small steps and knocked on the door, but there was no answer. Raul peered through the window, and noticed the lights weren't on.

'Maybe he's not home, let's try the back door.'

They followed him around and discovered it was unlocked. They walked inside and turned on the lights. Marina walked into the living room, and let out a terrifying scream. Raul and Luis rushed in to see what had happened. There was a dark figure standing in the room, so Luis flicked on the light. Standing in the living room with his sword pointed at Marina, was their Uncle Bruno.

'Marina! Raul! What are you doing here!?' he yelled.

'We came here to find you!' said Marina still squinting her eyes.

'Mind putting the sword away then?' asked Raul.

'Oh right! Sorry, where are my manners?' He leaned his sword against the wall and hugged the two of them. With his head on Raul's shoulder he noticed Luis standing there.

'Aren't you gonna introduce me?'

'Oh! Uncle Bruno - this is our friend Luis,' said Marina and pointed to him. He approached Luis and gave him a powerful handshake that shook his entire body.

'Nice to meet you.'

The moon medal dangling from Luis's neck shook a little and he noticed it immediately.

'Marina isn't this your chain? What's it doing on...wait is this how you got to the Island?'

'Yes, by accident Luis put on my medal, and like a miracle the moon started to work again,' replied Marina.

'This was no miracle, that medal is a powerful relic...that has the power to control the moon.'

Raul and Marina looked at each other in shock. Uncle Bruno looked up to the ceiling, and for a while he seemed lost in thoughts.

'I'm gonna make us all a drink, we have much to discuss, sit down,' he said.

He started coughing violently and walked to the kitchen. Luis took a seat and stared around the room. There were framed certificates and small weapons hanging on the walls, and above the fireplace was a huge eagle's head ornament. Luis was awe-struck at its realism.

Uncle Bruno shouted from the kitchen.

'So did you tell your friend about my past life!?'

Without even giving them time to respond, he answered his own question.

'I used to be a Knight for the Royal family of Adastra!'

Raul rolled his eyes like he'd heard this story a thousand times, but Luis was quite surprised.

'Our Uncle used to do battle for the King, he was the best skilled swordsman in the land,' said Raul.

Uncle Bruno came back into the room holding four mugs of hot chocolate.

'Was the best? I still am.'

He started coughing violently again, and spilled some of the drink on the floor.

'Excuse me kids.'

Marina looked up in concern.

'Uncle Bruno, are you alright?'

'I'm fine, it's just since this whole shadow madness, I've been feeling really weak. I think it affects us older folk more than you kids.'

Luis watched him and could sense he was putting on a brave face. He was extremely stocky and he had some battle scars on his cheeks.

'So does your father know you're here?'

'Dad was the one who told us to come see you,' said Raul.

'Coming all the way out here is no place for a couple of kids'.

'We're here because we want to find out what happened to the King,' said Marina.

'Do you know anything? Anything at all about his disappearance, or this strange shadow?' she asked.

After a long silence, their uncle finally spoke up.

'As far as I know the King was cursed.'

'Cursed!?' said a shocked Marina.

'All I remember is one day, when I was guarding the Kings room doing my duty patrolling the castle. I heard the King in a vicious argument, and then moments later I think I heard crying, but I wasn't sure who it was. I went down to the harbor to tell your father, and together we went back up. But the King's servant said he wasn't taking any visitors, and that we had to leave the Island immediately...if anyone knows what happened to the King, it would be Mr Plato, the King's assistant, and for all I know, he could have something do with this!'

The trio looked at each other intensely.

'But I'm not one to point the sword at anyone, truth is, no one really knows what happened. The whole thing is shrouded in darkness...literally.'

'How can we find Mr Plato?' asked Luis.

'Well Mr Plato lives on Emerald Bay Island - near Keplar Castle, but it's no use getting to him without the tide working.'

'But we fixed the tide!' said Marina excitedly.

'Fraid not, commend you on your achievements thus far, but all you kids did was activate a small portion of the moon's power. Keplar Castle is all the way on the other side of Adastra, and to get there you're gonna need all of the tide to be working.'

A stagnant silence filled the room, and the trio looked at one another hopelessly. As their uncle got out of his chair and warmed his hands by the fire, he looked up at his eagle statue hanging on the wall. Luis looked discouraged, but Uncle Bruno got everyone's attention, by knocking his fist on the eagles head.

'Out of all the animals, the eagle is by far my favourite.'

The trio looked at one another slowly - why was he talking about eagles?

'When the sky storms, and water begins to drench the land, do you know what the eagle does? It doesn't get scared by the cacophony of sounds, or go into hiding like the other birds...and it doesn't look for shelter like the land animals. The eagle is the only bird that uses the raging wind to soar high above the clouds, to avoid the torrential downpour.'

Luis, Marina, and Raul started to smile.

'You kids have shown tremendous courage by coming this far to see me, and I'm going to help you - like the eagle, to rise above the many storms of life. This being one of them.'

'So you know a way to get to the castle?' asked Raul.

'There is one other way, but its stab in the dark.'

Their uncle went into another room, and returned with a small book. It was quite dusty and tattered.

'I took this from the castle library one day...that's right

your Uncle does his fair share of reading, brains and the brawn me. Anyway, it contains some interesting facts and secrets about Adastra.'

The trio couldn't take their eyes of him as he flicked through the pages.

'Where is it? I know I read something in here about that medal of yours...ah here we go!'

He began reading a passage from the book.

'If the moon should ever fail, to restore the power sail to the isles, be brave, enter the caves, and in the shadows, seek the chains of light.'

They gathered round him, and he showed them a picture in the book. There was an illustration of a round circular pendant - entitled the moon medallion. The picture split into three separate diagrams and showed three necklaces with moon centerpieces. One of a quarter moon, another of a half moon, and lastly another crescent moon. Their uncle carried on reading.

'It says here that they were crafted in the light of the moon by the founders of this land, and they have the power to simulate the moon.'

Marina turned the page and noticed there was a map pinpointing the locations of each cave and chain. She took out her map and marked the points on it.

'Wow! One of the caves is on this exact Island...in the forest.' she added.

'Well we have to go and get it,' said Raul.

Their uncle shut the book and put it on the table. He looked at all three of them.

'Then you must go into the cave, retrieve that chain, and assemble the moon medallion.'

The three of them thanked him, and finished their drinks. They walked up to the door, but their uncle told them to wait. Coughing, he got up slowly and walked to the eagle head once more.

'I'd love to go with you guys, but I'm in no fit shape, and I'll probably be more of a hindrance.'

He opened the eagle's beak.

'Here I want you to take this with you,' and he drew out what looked like a sword.

'This is the Royal Blade of Adastra, it's the very blade I used to wield back when I was a fearless knight. I want you to carry it with you, no one knows what's lurking out in the forest now.'

Luis watched as Raul instantly stepped forward and grasped the blade.

'Thank you,' said Raul.

Their uncle walked the three of them to the door, and they stepped outside into the night.

'It was nice meeting you Luis.'

Luis flashed him a nervous smile, and the trio descended down the path, and into the forest. Their uncle shouted from the distance.

'Now go on! Be fearless, and throw caution...to return the wind to Adastra'

*

The forest was extremely dark, and the wind blocking density of the trees gave it an eerie feel. Luis looked around, he could tell that before the shadow had taken its course, the forest probably contained a plethora of creatures and wild life. Decomposing leaves fell off the trees as they ventured further, and Raul led the way hacking down the razor sharp thorns with the blade.

'Have you guys been in this forest before?' Luis asked curiously.

'When we were kids, we used to have picnics here, but never this far out. Going this far into the forest was always considered dangerous,' said Raul.

Time passed, and the forest got darker and more desolate, and the pathway that they were walking on had disappeared. The trees around them were breaking apart, and moss oozed from the trunks like decayed flesh. Luis didn't dare think how big the forest was, even the route they were taking had an incredible labyrinthine feel to it. Marina held Luis's hand, and he looked at her surprised.

'Walking through a dark forest, even though you haven't got a clue where you're going...it feels safer to hold someone's hand.'

Luis looked at her and smiled, but in front of him, Raul stopped moving.

'Marina have you got that map?' he asked.

She took it out from her pocket and gave it to him.

Raul looked confused.

'What's wrong?' asked Luis.

'The cave should be around here, but I can't see it.'

'We have to take in to account that the forest has probably evolved throughout the years,' said Marina.

Luis noticed something in the distance, covered by trees.

'The book said the relics are hidden in a cave, right? Then it has to be near that huge rock,' informed Luis.

'Hey, maybe you're right!' replied Raul.

Luis stamped on some bushes and made a pathway. As they walked toward the rock they noticed the ground beneath them started to sink in.

'Be careful this area is like a swamp!' yelled Raul.

He drew the blade and sliced a tall branch from the tree, using it for leverage in the spongy tract. The everglade got deeper and deeper as they walked through, but eventually they reached the rock. Raul hacked away at some branches, and spotted a small hole, enough for one person at a time to squeeze through.

'This has to be it,' said Raul.

They each took some deep breaths and crawled through the hole, Raul going first. Inside the cave, they looked up and noticed there was no roof, and the sky above was providing just enough light to see.

'It looks like this could have been some sort of volcanic rock, like an old dormant volcano,' expressed Marina.

'Any sign of that moon medal?' asked Raul, as he scanned the area. Luis noticed two large rocks at the end of the cave. He tried to push it aside, but it was too heavy. He called the others over, and all three exerted their force on to it. Slowly the top rock fell over, breaking into pieces. Raul kicked the remaining rock to the side - It was covering a tunnel entrance. A damp smell spewed outward, and Luis spotted something on the ground.

'Look there's some sort of silver box on the floor.'

'That's got to be it! Luis you're the one who spotted it, you do the honors,' said Raul happily.

Luis approached the box, and knelt down. He opened up the hinged lid, and inside was a small golden quarter moon on a gold chain. He lifted it up and walked back toward the others - with a huge smile on his face. Marina smiled back, but suddenly her smile transitioned into a look of intense fear!

'Luis look out!' she screamed at the top of her lungs.

Raul quickly drew the blade. Luis turned around and fell to the floor in fright. He looked up, in front of him was a knight - wearing silver armor, and wielding a huge axe. His face was hidden and protected by a helmet, and his gauntlets covered in black spikes. Luis looked at him, and was instantly overcome with fear. The knight glared at Marina and Raul, and turned his attention to Luis, who was still on the floor. He stamped on Luis's leg – stopping him from moving, and raised his gigantic axe in the air. Luis trembled with fear, and shut his eyes. Raul threw a rock at the knight's head, but its helmet deflected it with ease. The knight slowly turned his face toward Raul.

'Let him go now!' yelled Raul and he pointed the blade at him.

'So it is you, who wishes to die?' The knight said in a horrible husky voice.

The knight kicked Luis aside, and he hit the rocky wall. He slowly got up, and looked at his now grazed and bleeding elbows.

'Marina, Luis, stay to the side of the wall! Stand up as straight as you can, so you don't get hit by his axe!' said Raul with conviction.

The knight charged at Raul and swung his giant axe at his body. Raul swiftly managed to duck under his vicious swipes, and he replied back with a medley of punches and sword strikes. Luis noticed on the knight's shoulder panel was the royal insignia, the same one that was flapping about on Raul's cape. The knight, swinging round in circles with his axe, backed Raul into a corner. He charged at Raul, and gaining a serious momentum, swung! Raul ducked again - missing the axe by an inch. The knight's axe had gotten stuck in the rock. Raul crawled around him and sensing this as his chance began striking the knights body armor with the blade. The knight's chest and back panels fell off, and Raul realized the knight wasn't human - his body a gaseous jet black. Raul, shocked and scared at the sight, dropped his guard. The knight turned around and grasped Raul's throat and held him up in the air. His hands were icy cold, and his grip tightened around his fragile neck. Raul let out a painful scream, and dropped the blade to the floor. Luis and Marina watched on in horror, as Raul looked at them frantically.

'Luis pick up the sword! Cut him where his armor isn't protecting him,' wheezed Raul.

Marina screamed at Luis and told him to pick up the blade! Luis cautiously walked into the arena and picked up the weapon.

'Luis now, strike him now!' ordered Raul - his feet now kicking air for sweet release. Luis's hand shook rapidly as he walked up to the hideous being.

'Luis please! Hit him with the sword!' yelled Marina.

Raul's eyes turned crimson, and his kicking became more violent. Luis raised the sword, and his whole body

trembled with fear. But the knight had seen enough.
'Life will tolerate nervousness, but when you don't act,
life will punish you for hesitancy!' declared the knight.
His cruel voice rattled Luis, and he dropped the blade.
The knight lifted Raul up higher, and with one
powerful concentrated blow, gashed his heart with his
black spiked gauntlets. Raul coughed up a dark blood,
and the knight dropped him to the rocky floor. Marina
let out a huge scream that echoed
painfully around the mountain. She ran up to her
brother, and knelt down beside him. The knight
laughed, and picked off some of Raul's ripped shirt that
was on his gauntlets. Not perceiving the kids a threat he
turned around to retrieve his axe stuck in the wall. Luis
looked down at Raul - who seemed mortally wounded.
He became extremely angry with himself, and picked
up the blade once more. He charged at the knight, and
stuck the blade right into his back. The knight turned
around and let out a huge dark cry.
'You don't have long until he becomes infected,' rasped
knight.
His gaseous body started to disappear.
'You may have defeated me, but this is just a pyrrhic
victory, soon darkness will eclipse the land and you'll all
join us!'
Suddenly he evaporated like smoke and trailed off into
the sky. Luis fell down to his knees, and looked at Raul,

who was breathing heavily. His shirt had huge tear marks, like it had been savaged by the claw of a lion.

'I'm sorry Raul, I'm so sorry!' cried Luis.

'Don't worry Luis, it's not your fault.'

Raul was hurt, and even though he wanted to close his eyes in pain, he resisted.

'We have to get him help!' said Marina, 'We have to take him back to our uncle.'

Luis got up and walked to the cave entrance.

'I'll go out first, and pull Raul through the hole.'

He crawled out, and Marina slowly edged Raul near the hole, from the other end Luis grabbed his legs and yanked him out.

*

Luis and Marina both supporting Raul's arms on their respective shoulders, walked back through the forest, as fast as they could.

'I'm sorry Marina, I just got scared,' said Luis

Marina didn't respond, and together they carried the injured Raul through the forestation. After a long walk back, they finally exited the forest. Dragging Raul up the steps to their uncle's house, Marina harshly banged on the door. Luis looked at Raul, who was slowly losing consciousness. Their uncle opened the door.

'He's hurt! Uncle Bruno you have to do something

please!' shouted Marina.

He looked at Raul and saw the three gaping wounds on his chest, and instantly helped Luis bring him inside. He cleared his table, took off Raul's cape, and laid him down slowly. Luis and Marina watched on nervously as their uncle brought out a supply of medical equipment. He dabbed Raul's chest with a salt water sponge.

'This should clean up any infections,' he said calmly.

'What happened out there guys?'

An awkward silence filled the room, and Luis spoke up.

'After finding the quarter moon medal, a Knight appeared and hurt Raul, but it was my fault, I should have protected him, he begged me to protect him.'

Uncle Bruno looked at Luis. 'A knight?'

'He was wielding this axe, and was heavily guarded in armor,' sobbed Luis.

Marina's uncle didn't say anything and focused his attention on Raul's wound.

'Now this might hurt a bit Raul, bear with me.'

He took out a white soft pad and applied a small amount of pressure to his chest. Raul sprung up and started to breathe heavily.

'Calm down Raul! Everything's gonna be fine, I need you to relax.'

He removed the pad from Raul's chest and stood there in shock.

'What? How is that possible?' said Uncle Bruno.

Marina looked up at him. 'What! What's happened?'
Her uncle showed her the pad - there was no blood on
it at all. He turned to face Luis.
'Luis this knight did he injure Raul with his weapon?'
'Err no, he was wearing these spikes on his wrists.'
Marina's uncle pointed to his wrists. 'His gauntlets?'
'Yeah,' said Luis.
Raul started shaking on the table, with his hand - he
signaled Luis to come closer.
'Luis please don't feel guilty because I got hurt, it was
my own fault for being careless. When he slashed me
with his dark armor, it felt like he infected me with
something…I can feel myself getting weaker.'
Raul grabbed Luis's hand and squeezed it.
'You have to finish what we started, find the other
moon medals,' he whispered.
He squeezed Luis's hand, and closed his eyes. Marina,
seeing her brother in pain started crying. Luis felt
Raul's hand become extremely cold, and he let it go.
'What's happened to him?' asked Marina.
'There's nothing I could do Marina, these lacerations
can't be healed by any medical instruments,' said Uncle
Bruno. He wiped away her tears, and put his arm on
her shoulder.
'We should count ourselves lucky that these weren't real
wounds by that axe, otherwise he wouldn't have made
it.'

'Will he be okay?' asked Luis.

'Leave him here with me, my nephew's strong like his uncle.'

He noticed Marina was still shaken up, and told her to get some fresh air. Marina walked out slowly, and Luis heard the front door slam shut.

'Let her get some time to herself. Looking at the ocean should calm her down,' said Uncle Bruno.

Luis just continued to stare at the lifeless Raul on the table.

'Bruno how have you remained so calm?' asked Luis.

'This is nothing. I've seen a lot worse in my time. Back in the day, hundreds of us would go into battle. I'd see friends and loved ones get hurt all the time. After years of exposure, your mind just gets used to it, and you learn to deal with the adversity.'

Marina's uncle looked at Luis square in the eyes.

'You can't go blaming yourself for what happened, Raul even said it was his fault for putting you in such a challenging predicament.'

'I just feel bad for not doing anything.'

'Well if you didn't do anything, who defeated the knight? Coz I know it wasn't my niece.'

'I did. I used your blade.'

It started to dawn on Luis that even though he hesitated at first, he still did something useful.

'My blade?'

'Yes the blade you gave to Raul.'

'Luis that blade is yours now, you heard Raul, you have to continue on with your mission.'

Uncle Bruno sensed that Luis was still unsure of himself, he told him to pick up the blade and hold it high in the air. Luis wrapped his fingers round the hilt and held it skyward. Uncle Bruno cleared his throat, and told Luis to shut his eyes.

'You have a father Luis, and if you trace your heritage up throughout the years, you'll find an unbroken line of fathers and sons. Now your forefathers faced all kinds of adversity. Wars of unmatched scale and ferocity, and horrible famines, but during all of this your fathers had the courage to create...that bloodline can be traced to you. Now imagine the soldiers that stood alongside your ancestors, the unfortunate ones who didn't survive - their line died out, but yours survived. That means cultivating in your body, is the blood of warriors, winners, and champions! Now whenever you wield your blade, I want you to remember Raul. I want you to remember your blood. I want you to remember your legacy!'

Luis opened his eyes and a surge of confidence flowed through his body. Marina's uncle could sense the impact of his powerful words.

'You see, you already have this warrior mentality deep inside you, all you have to do is bring it to the surface.

Now go out there and find the other moon relics, and if any knights appear, slay them!'

'Thank you,' said Luis graciously.

Luis and Uncle Bruno walked to the stony beach, and found Marina sitting down near the shore.

'Raul is gonna stay here with me, he needs to rest.' said Uncle Bruno.

He outstretched his hand, Marina pulled herself up, dusting the sand off her clothes.

'Raul's gonna pull through Marina, don't you worry.'

Marina glanced at Luis - who seemed completely different. His body language was more powerful than before, and the blade was sheathed in a scabbard around his waist. Luis pulled the quarter moon medal from his pocket, and Uncle Bruno watched on eagerly.

'I wanna see this for my own eyes.'

The three of them stood by the shore and looked out toward the Sea of Serenity. It looked like it was cut in two halves - one side moving perfectly, and the other completely still. Luis attached the medal to the crescent moon pendant on his chain. A loud rumble blasted through the air - and the ground beneath them started to shake. The fragmented moon above them started to converge, and slowly the dark cracks vanished. A fluorescent light shimmered down toward the ocean, and it started to sway once more. The sound of the ocean waves startled Uncle Bruno. Luis and Marina looked up at him, and watched as his face filled with wonder, love, and gratitude.

'Sometimes you forget how calming the sound of the ocean is,' he exclaimed.

They all stared at the ocean for a few minutes, and after a while Uncle Bruno went inside, returning with Raul's cape, and the book.

'Luis I think you should wear this. That way Raul can be with you two in spirit.'

Luis smiled as he fastened the cape around his neck - a snug fit.

'And Marina this is for you, I'm sure it will come in handy on your travels.'

Uncle Bruno handed the book to Marina, and she put it in her bag. Luis's spotted the royal insignia on the cape and instantly had a flashback of the knight in the cave.

'Bruno do you have any idea why the knight had royal armor on?'

'Hmm that is strange…did he mention anything about the King?'

'No, I don't think so.'

Uncle Bruno stared at the moon, thinking of a plausible reason.

'Sorry Luis but I haven't got a clue. But if this darkness is slowly engulfing people, and if these knights are willing to hurt the innocent , then you two are gonna have to put a stop to it. All the more reason for you to get to Keplar Castle as quick as you can.'

'Well we can't waste any more time,' said Luis.

Marina took out the map, and showed her uncle the next marked location.

'Looks like the next medal is on Sparkling Coral Island. You're gonna have to sail approximately three miles north east, and you should find it,' said Uncle Bruno.

Luis went ahead and pushed the boat into the water.

'I want you both to take good care of each other, okay?' They both looked at each other and silently acknowledged his wise words. Luis went over and shook his hand.

'Thank you, for everything...I promise I won't let you down.'

Marina hugged her uncle and squeezed him tight.

'Take good care of my brother.'

'I'm proud of both of you, chin up, and keep fighting!' He smiled to himself, and waved them goodbye, as they sailed off toward Sparkling Coral Island. But unexpectedly a thought flashed into Uncle Bruno's mind, and a worried look took over his face. He waved his hands in the air, and desperately tried to get their attention, but it was too late...their small sea vessel had sailed off into the dark nebulous ocean.

CHAPTER FOUR

Masquerading The Moonlight

"Thirst drove me down to the water where I drank the moon's reflection"

- Rumi

They had been travelling for hours, much longer then Luis had initially forecasted, and as the small sailboat bobbed up and down on the water, Luis began to sense that something strange was going on. He took out the compass that Marina's father had given him. The dial was spinning out of control, and he looked at it confusion.

'It feels like we've been sailing around in circles,' puffed Marina.

'It's weird I know, but it's this damn compass,' explained Luis.'

'A poor workman blames his tools,' said Marina.

Luis showed her the compass, but she ignored him and looked out toward the ocean. There was an inelegant atmosphere on the boat, stemming from Marina hardly speaking since they had departed. Her thoughts that Luis had now gotten them lost, augmented her beliefs, that he wasn't right for the job. Luis in frustration threw the compass in the sea. A small flash of light flickered in the water, and for a few moments he wondered if his mind was playing tricks on him. They carried on sailing forward and after a while Luis noticed they were directly under the moon. He looked up and inspected the black fractures that had proliferated its vanilla surface, and he pondered what it previously looked like, before it met with its ill fate. As time passed, Luis tried to make conversation with Marina, but she only responded in murmurs. He studied the map and slowly changed the ship's direction.

'We should arrive on the Island soon,' said Luis.

Marina still ignored him.

'What's Sparkling Coral Island like?' he asked in a curious tone.

Marina said nothing. Growing tired of her silent treatment, Luis decided to confront her. He hopped down from the rudder, and sat right in front of her.

'Are you just going to ignore me for the whole journey? Marina, how many times do you want me to apologize?'

Without giving him eye contact she spoke.

'Why did you lie to my uncle?'

'What do you mean? I never lied to your uncle.'

'Yes you did.'

Luis tried to speak but she spoke up first.

'You shouldn't make promises you can't keep! When we were leaving the Island, you promised my uncle that you weren't going to let him down.'

'Yeah, but I haven't had a chance to prove myself.'

'You had your chance, back in that cave, and you blew it!'

Marina turned to face him, and Luis noticed her eyes were filled with water.

'This whole boat ride, I've been thinking, maybe this whole journey has been a big mistake. You couldn't even protect my brother when he begged you!'

Luis lowered his head.

'An now I'm scared that you're gonna let something dangerous happen to me.'

A small tear fell down the side of her cheek, and Luis caught it with his knuckle.

'Marina, I know it sounds like I'm making excuses, but I'm not. You heard what your brother said...it was his fault. I've apologized so much, and now I'm trying to put it right. You know, I've never done anything like this before. What's worse is, I could die out here and no one back home would even realize. Has it not occurred to you that I'm scared as well?'

Marina was taken aback by his tone.

'I'm scared that I might not see my parents again, I'm scared that I might not get to fulfill my dream. I'll admit when Raul stepped up and took your uncle's blade, I thought it was plain sailing...but now I'm holding the blade, and I promise I'm going to make things right.'

She looked at Luis and felt comfort in his words.

'And I always keep my promises Marina.'

'That's the first time I've ever heard you say anything with such conviction,' said Marina.

She put her hand over his.

'I'm sorry too. I shouldn't have given you such a hard time. When I'm upset I have a tendency for taking it out on others around me.'

There was a long silence, but this time it wasn't awkward. The pair of them just acknowledged each other's presence.

'You mentioned before, that you were scared you might not be able to fulfill your dreams?'

Luis looked up at her slowly.

'What are your dreams Luis?' she asked.

Luis smiled at her.

'My dream has always been to visit the moon.'

'You mean, like an astronaut?'

'Yeah. I'm still learning more about it, but I love astronomy, I love looking at the moon and the stars.'

Luis wanted to tell her about his parents, and their

views on the matter, but he didn't think Marina would be able to relate.

'That's beautiful…I can't wait for you to see the moon in Adastra back to its shining best,' responded Marina.

'What about you, you must have dreams as well?'

'Of course! One day I'm going to be an oceanographer.'

'What's that?' asked Luis.

'Someone who studies the sea!'

Luis leaned in curiously.

'When I was little my dad used to take me fishing in his boat, I would spend hours watching the waves lap the rocks, and seeing all the different fish my dad would catch. I used to come home and you could smell the sea in my hair.'

Marina put her hand in the ocean and cupped some of the water.

'I'll never forget one day, some of the other kids in my class poked fun at me, about my infatuation with the ocean. I remember running home crying, and Raul comforted me. He gave me an oyster that he'd found on the beach. He told me to imagine myself as the pearl, and he compared himself as the shell - always there to protect me.'

Her words really sunk in, and he compared her situation with the relationship between his parents. He had never anticipated that Marina had gone through hardships related to her dream. They both sat there and thought about their dreams, and after a while Marina spoke up.

'You know, maybe everything does happen for a reason' expressed Marina.

'How so?' asked Luis.

'Maybe Raul was meant to get hurt.'

 Luis looked confused.

'You see, your dream is related to the moon, and my dream related to the ocean. Two forces that work together, and when they're combined, they have a subtle power to move us all...if one isn't in harmony with the other, they don't operate at their best. Maybe it was supposed to be me and you…who save Adastra.' Luis looked at her in amazement - it was a beautiful correlation that made so much sense.

*

They were now just meters away from Sparkling Coral Island. Luis spotted a small skyline, and gleaned that the isle had a small cityscape structure. He veered the boat toward the Islands small beach and closed the sail. He hopped out first and tied the boat to the boardwalk. As Marina stepped out of the boat, she spotted something flash underneath the water's surface, almost like a bolt of lightning. She peered over the edge of the boat, but couldn't see anything.

'Everything okay?' asked Luis.

Marina brushed it off as nothing, and jumped out. They walked down the boardwalk, and Luis noticed that it was much sturdier compared to the one on Oasis Island. There was a small beach house at the end of the path, and as they walked closer, someone inside the house turned off all the lights.

'Did you just see that?' asked Luis.

'Yeah, how strange.' said Marina.

Luis clambered up the steps, and knocked on the front door. But no one answered.

'They're ignoring us,' said Luis.

'I'm sure there's other places we can try,' said Marina.

Coming to the end of the beach, they both looked up and were taken back by the architectural design of the small beach town. The pair walked through the derelict roads, and it soon became clear that no one was around. The darkness emitting from above the rooftops gave the town a forsaken feel. They reached the end of the road and noticed there was no sign of a cave. Marina looked through the map and scratched her head in confusion.

'I've never been to this Island before, but my instincts are telling me we're not gonna find a cave around here.'

'Do you think the map is wrong?' asked Luis.

'This whole place just seems odd,' replied Marina.

'Yeah I do get the feeling something, or someone, is watching us.'

'Maybe we should look around in some of the shops, and houses, and see if we can find any clues,' said Marina.

Luis looked up at the dark clouds.

'Well we can't stay out here for too long, or we'll risk exposure to that infectious fog.'

Luis looked around, the shop signs were dusty and they dangled off their hinges. It was clear that the economic activity that had supported the Island had ceased. Marina spotted a shop that didn't look too dilapidated, and as she approached the front door she realized it was open. They walked in slowly, and the bell above the door rung. An elderly woman's voice shouted from behind the counter.

'Who's there?!'

'Err, my name's Marina, I'm from Oasis Island.'

The elderly woman peered out from behind the door.

'Who's he?'

'My names Luis.'

'What do you want?' The old woman said in a rasping tone.

'We don't mean you any harm, we just want to ask you some questions about the island,' said Marina.

She spotted Luis's sword, around his waist.

'Tell the boy to wait outside, and I'll come out,' with

her finger she pointed to his weapon.

Marina realized what she was referring to, and whispered to Luis.

'She thinks you might be a threat, because of your sword. Go wait outside.'

'Are you sure?'

'Yes I'll be fine, go.'

Luis walked out off the shop and shut the door behind him. The old woman appeared from the back room. She had long grey hair, and a slight hunchback. Marina shook her hand and shuddered as it was unusually cold. The old woman looked at her longingly.

'My! You're just a young girl...I'm sorry for all that before, we haven't had any customers in a while, and with all the strange happenings you never can be too sure'.

'Miss...'

The old woman interrupted Marina.

'You can call me Catharina,' said the old woman, now smiling. Marina took the map out of her pocket.

'Catharina, do you know where we can find this place here?'

She watched the woman's eyes scan the paper and noticed they had huge, unnatural dark circles around them.

'It looks like some sort of cave?'

Marina lit up.

'Yes, yes it is! Do you know where we can find it?'

The old woman paused for a few moments.

'No I don't, I'm sorry,'

'Do you know anyone that would know where to find it? It's just that we've looked everywhere and no one's around.'

'My husband would have known, but he's come down with a terrible illness recently.'

'I'm sorry to hear that, what happened?'

'He used to work over on Emerald Bay Island, and as you can imagine that hideous fog got inside of his body and started making him feel ill. The worst part is now it's taking over this Island as well. We're all feeling the effects of it.'

'I hope he gets better,' wished Marina.

Not wanting to waste any more time, she thanked her and walked to the door.

'Wait!' the old woman cried. 'I don't know how you two kids got here or why you're looking for dark caves, but if you want to find anything on this Island, your best chance is to find Núria.'

'Núria lives on this Island? I've heard my parents speak of her a few times.'

'Núria is the guardian of this Island, but I haven't seen her in a while. Head back toward the beach. There's a house with a green door. Knock on the door three times, wait three seconds, and then knock twice.' Marina watched as the old woman mimicked her actions with her fist on the counter. 'There's a family living there who might be able to help you.'

Marina smiled to herself.

'Thank you miss, I'm sure your husband will get better soon!'

'You're welcome my dear, be careful now, and good luck'.

Marina walked outside.

'Well did you find out anything?' asked Luis.

'Looks like we're heading back to the beach' said Marina.

'Why? We already tried there?'

'Yes, but we didn't use the password!'

'Password?'

'Don't worry I'll explain on the way down.'

Back on the beach, they walked up the steps to the house with the green door.

'Are you sure this is the right one? We already tried this place,' asked Luis.

Marina noticed the lights were still off.

'It has to be, she did say green door, now we just have to knock on the door in a certain way.'

Marina knocked on the door making sure to use the specific pattern. There was a long wait, and Marina started to wonder if she used the correct sequence.

The sound of a bolt being unlocked filled the silence, and slowly the door opened. A pair of eyes behind the door looked at them and, after a few seconds it opened wider. Luis, and Marina walked in, and the person shut the door very quickly, and flicked on a light. They looked up and saw a tall man. Staring at them strangely, he bellowed down the hall.

'I was right dear! It's two kids.'

He looked back down at them,

'Come in sit down.'

He led them into the front room, and pulled out some chairs for them to sit by the fire.

'So where are you two from?'

'We're from Oasis Island,' Marina explained.

He shouted down the hall again, Luis scrunched in his chair not expecting the bellow.

'There from Oasis dear!'

A tall woman entered the room with a plate full of small sandwiches, cut into small triangles.

'Would you stop your incessant yelling, the kids in the next room are trying to sleep.'

He took a sandwich from the plate, and gestured at the pair 'Help yourselves.'

'Thanks,' said Luis taking a handful.

'How did a couple of kids like you get to the Island then?'

His wife took a seat and listened in.

'Well the tide connecting Aquatic Reef to Sparkling Coral Island is working, so we sailed here,' said Marina. The man looked at them confused.

'I thought you said you were from Oasis?'

'Oh! We are, it's just we're trying to get to Keplar Castle and we travelled here from Aquatic Reef.'

'Ah I see.'

'We met Catharina, she told us how to knock on your door,' said Marina.

His wife looked at them shocked.

'That was you two earlier? I'm so sorry! It's just with all the creepy goings on, you don't know who could be at the door. For several months people on this Island have been using a sort of password for each other.' she explained.

The woman offered them a drink, but Marina knowing they couldn't stay long got straight to the point.

'We were wondering if you could help us find Núria?'

'You and me both!' said the man. 'No one's seen her in months, and since she's been gone the Island's had no electricity. We can barely operate.'

'So you've met her before?' asked Marina.

'Of course, everyone here knows Núria. How do you think the Island got its name?

'How did the Island get its name?' asked Luis.

'Núria is the friendly electric eel that powers the Island,' he added. Luis looked at Marina shocked, but she nudged him to stay quiet. The man and his wife stared at each other in thought, and Marina noticed they both had similar dark patches under their eyes. The darkness must be affecting all the Islanders she thought. After a few moments his wife spoke, and there was a sadness in her voice.

'We have two boys aged five and six and our youngest, James, used to be fond with Núria.'

'Do you think he could help us find her?' asked Marina.

'It's just he's been really ill for months now, and recently he's just been sleeping all day. He's breathing normally, but now I'm starting to get a little worried.'

'Aren't there any doctors around?' asked Luis.

'All the doctors live on Emerald Bay Island, so no, there aren't any close by,' said her husband.

'Come on, I'll take you to them, maybe his brother might know something,' she said.

Marina and Luis followed her upstairs into the bedroom. The woman opened the door. Her two sons were in the room. One of them was playing with his toys on the floor, and the other was sleeping on a bed near the window. Luis watched the youngest child as he played without a care in the world – for a second Luis felt sorry for him. The boy was so young, and unsuspecting of the current dangers. But it also made him want to fight on, and help the people of Adastra.

'Is that James over there?' asked Luis, and he pointed

to the boy sleeping.

His mom nodded. The moon could be seen from the window, its dim luminescent light inconspicuously shone through the curtains. Luis knelt down beside him, and the light from the moon gently bounced off his medal and onto the small child's face, similar to the reflection of a buttercup under someone's chin. All of a sudden the child gently opened his eyes. His mom stood there in disbelief. Luis smiled at her - unbeknown to what he'd done. The small child rubbed his eyes and sat up in the bed. He was wearing dungarees like his older brother.

'Hey my name's Luis, and this is my friend Marina.' The boy looked at her and adjusted his eyes.

'We need your help, we're going to see the King in Keplar Castle, but before we can, we need to meet with his friend Núria. And your mom told us, you're good friends with her.'

The boy yawned and stretched his hands wide.

'I would always find her by the boardwalk. I used to throw pebbles in the water and she would surface,' he said softly. His mom looked at him and started smiling she couldn't believe her son was awake and speaking again.

'Thanks buddy,' said Luis happily.

The boy climbed out of his bed and started playing with his brother.

'I don't know how you did it, but thank you so much,' said the woman.

They walked to the front door, and the couple thanked, and wished them luck for their journey. Back on the beach Luis scooped up some pebbles with his hands, and together him and Marina walked to the end of the boardwalk to summon Núria. Luis threw the stones in the ocean consecutively, but nothing happened. Suddenly Marina realized something.

'Luis, where's our boat gone!?'

He looked down at the rope, and saw it had been cut in half.

'There it is!' Luis noticed the boat, floating underneath the boardwalk.

'I think I'll be able to reach it, hold onto my legs, so I don't fall in.' said Marina.

She leaned over the edge, and tried to grasp the other end of the rope attached to the boat. Luis, with his body weight on Marina's legs, raised her down lower.

She snagged the rope, pulled the boat out from under, and hopped in.

'I'll bring the boat round to the shore so this doesn't happen again,' said Marina.

But all of a sudden something leapt out of the water. It had a huge purple cylindrical body, and discharged an instantaneous flash of light. The eel like creature snarled at Luis, as it crashed back down into the water –

consequencing a huge wave. It opened its mouth and clamped onto the piece of rope. Marina screamed at Luis to help. The eel sank below the surface. Sensing what was about to happen, Luis sprinted to the edge of the boardwalk and jumped off. He landed in the boat just in time, before it sped off. The boat whizzed across the shore at an alarming speed. Marina's knuckles turned white as she held onto the rudder desperately. Luis managed to stand up slowly, and by holding on to the boats seats, made his way to the front to look over the small bow. Something was flashing underneath the water's surface.

'Luis you have to do something!' yelled Marina.

He grabbed onto the rope but a surge of electricity travelled up and shocked him. He shrieked in pain and fell to the boat floor, grabbing his hand. The boat turned around and speeded toward the coast.

'Luis look, it's heading straight for the huge rocks near the shore!'

The boat zipped toward the boardwalk, and he quickly thought of an idea.

'Whatever it is that's trying to kill us, it's going to try and ram us into the rocks! Marina, put all your body weight to the left of the boat, when we reach the boardwalk grab onto my legs!' said Luis.

The boat veered toward the left and approached the boardwalk at incredible speed. Luis detached the sail, as it got closer.

'Now!' screamed Luis. In one quick swipe he cut the rope with his sword and penetrated the wooden boardwalk with the blade. Marina grabbed onto his legs and together they hung underneath the wooden plank from the blades hilt. The boat crashed onto the sandy shore, and the eel smashed into the rocks with terminal velocity! Luis pulled the blade out from the plank, and they both fell into the sea, and swam to the shore. Drenched in water they walked along the sandy beach, and to the rocks, but the eel wasn't there. Suddenly a huge blue electric blast came out from the water and nearly struck the pair's feet. Falling back they shuffled back to their boat and leaned it upward - using it as a shield.

'This is the friendly eel!?' said Luis, as he brushed away some seaweed stuck on his shoulder.

Marina peered from behind the boat, and looked at Núria who was attacking them from the low-tide coastline.

'Something's different. This can't be the same Núria, her face looks completely different. Like she's been possessed,' said Marina.

Another bolt of electricity smacked the boat.

'We have to do something quick Marina! We're soaking wet, one hit of that electricity and we're dead,' said Luis.

Marina looked up at the moon and saw its light shining on the sea's surface. She remembered what happened to the little boy, who snapped out of his dark illness from the moonlight's reflection.

'Luis, I have an idea. That little boy who woke up when he saw you. It was because off the moonlight reflecting of the medal. I'm gonna distract Núria, and I need you to get into the water and reflect the moonlight onto her face.'

Luis un-tucked the medal from inside his shirt.

'Are you sure this will work?'

'We have no choice,' said Marina, as she moved into a crouching position. 'Go now!'

Marina sprung to her feet and ran towards the boardwalk. Núria locked onto her shooting a bolt of electricity but missing by fractions. Sand blasted up into the air and Luis sprinted toward the rocks, and crept into the water.

'Hurry!' yelled Marina, as she dodged another onslaught of electricity. Luis, now tiptoeing in the water with his chin at the surface, moved into the light. He put the medal into the water, and tried to bounce the light onto Núria, but its surface area wasn't big enough. Núria let out a high pitched scream and charged up another round.

'Use the blade Luis!' shouted Marina.

Luis drew the blade, but the sound alerted Núria and

she quickly turned around. Luis tilted the blade and bounced the moonlight on to Núria's face. Her small eyes squinted as she let out a deafening screech piercing Luis's ears. He climbed out of the water, and Núria sprawled out onto the shallow sea. Marina walked closer to her, and saw her purple body was no longer recklessly producing volts of electricity. She put her hand on the eel's face.

'Núria?'

'Be careful Marina,' expressed Luis.

Núria coiled inward and moved back into the water, and resurfaced near the boardwalk. After getting their breath back, they walked to the boardwalk to meet her.

'Saved by two adolescents,' said Núria in a surprising tone.

Luis looked stunned - he didn't know Núria could speak. She turned to Marina.

'You I recognise your face, you're the fisherman's daughter.'

Marina nodded, and Núria turned to face Luis.

'You're not from this place are you?'

'No, how can you tell? asked Luis.

'I've never seen a more shocked face.'

Núria shuddered and small droplets of water scattered through the air like a sprinkler.

'I must apologize. The darkness that looms above infiltrated my beautiful Island. Soon it infected the water, and every living thing in it, including myself,' said Núria. 'How can I repay you two for saving me?'

'We need to ask you a question about the Island,' said Marina.

'I know all that there is on this Island, ask away.'

Marina took out the map and showed it to her.

'We need to find this cave here, we've searched all the Island and had no luck. Do you know where we can find it?'

Núria without looking at the map spoke.

'The cave you seek, is located behind the Island, it can only be reached by boat.'

'No wonder we couldn't find it,' said Marina.

'However the caves on this Island are shrouded in pitch black darkness, and you face extreme danger if your vision is restricted,' warned Núria.

'Is there any way we can light the cave?' asked Luis.

'Have you forgotten who you're speaking with child? I am Núria, the one who lights the land.'

Luis looked up at her cautiously.

'I will come with you and light the path,' said Núria.

'Wow, thank you!' exclaimed Marina.

They ran back to the beach, and Luis pushed the boat out to sea. Knowing that it was safe to travel, they sailed with Núria to the back of the Island.

*

Luckily the boat hadn't sustained too much damage, and was still able to sail. Luis wringed his cape dry, as they followed Núria toward the Island's rocky exterior. Marina spotted the small dark sea cave at the base of the cliffs. Luis changed the ship's course, and they entered the dark chasm. The cave just like Núria said, was pitch black. Luis couldn't even see his hands in the darkness, and he grabbed onto the cold weathered rock for grip. Nuria let out a low pitched screech, and lit the cave with an array of blue hued light. Luis climbed on to the raised level of rocks, and pulled Marina up with him.

'I shall wait here for you,' said Núria.

They thanked her and walked down deep into the cave. It was incredibly quiet, and you could hear water droplets from above dripping down. The cold air forced them both to shiver, and they jumped from one rock to another, advancing more forward. They reached a dead end, and Luis slapped the rock wall with his palm, to see if was protecting another hole like last time. He pressed his ear against the rock, and heard the sound of cascading water coming from the other side.

'Something's on the other side of this wall,' he remarked...we have to find a way through.'

There was a huge circular patch of coral on the ground,

Marina stuck her hand in, and realized it was covering a huge hole of water. Luis drew his blade, and cut away the coral, revealing a tunnel.

'That's how we get to the other side,' said Marina.

She dived in without hesitating and swam into the hole. Luis looked through the water, it was dark and narrow and he hated things that made him feel claustrophobic. He took a deep breath, dived in, and swam through. There was a dim light on the other side and he resurfaced. Luis climbed out and looked around - he was on the opposite side of the cave. There was a tiny hole atop the rocks letting just enough light in for visibility. Marina was standing in front of a small cave - with water trickling down its roof.

'This has to be it,' she said.

He poked the blade into the cave and let the water run down its silvery surface. He walked inside, and saw a small chrome coloured box with the royal insignia on its surface.

'Be careful!' yelled Marina.

He knelt down and opened the box - and resting on top of the black velvet padding was the Half-moon medal. Luis quickly put the chain into his pocket, and walked backward gripping his blade.

'I've got it Marina, I'm walking out now.' But suddenly something knocked him backward out of the cave with huge force. He stumbled backward, and Marina managed to catch him.

'We have to go now!' yelled Luis.

He grabbed her hand and they rushed to the pool of water. They could hear the heavy clanking of metal armor slowly coming at them. Luis in the corner of his eye saw something flying toward them, and shielded Marina. Two daggers flew into the wall, and penetrated the rock. Luis, remembering Raul's words instructed Marina to crouch in the corner. He tightened his grip on the blade's handle, and turned to face the knight. It looked similar to the one in the Aquatic Reef cave - protected by heavy armor, with a face concealed by a metal helmet. Luis looked at his gauntlets, but they weren't spiked.

'Foolish child, how dare you medal with royal affairs. Return the relic,' he snarled.

Luis just stared at him. Not being able to match the knight's rasping voice to a face intensified his macabre image. The knight produced a huge black spiked flail, and spun it in mid-air, building momentum.

'Luis watch out for its black spikes! They're similar to the ones that hurt Raul!' screamed Marina.

Luis's watched the knight's movements with incredible focus. The knight unleashed the flail, and Luis quickly dodged it. It crashed into the rock wall, and obliterated the surface. The knight yanked it out, and began swinging it again. Luis recited Uncle Bruno's speech to inspire him, but he was still shaking in fear. The knight swung the flail once more, Luis lifting the blade parried the long chain, and forced the knight to miss, causing immense damage to the rocky cave. Luis wanted to get in close to attack him, but the little voice in his head stopped him. The knight in his peripheral vision saw Marina meters away from him, in perfect striking distance. He moved toward her and swung his death-dealing flail in the air. Marina screamed and clamped her eyes shut. Luis sensed she was in grave danger, and ran up to the knight, barging him into the pool of water. The knight soaking wet, climbed out and grabbed Luis. He raised him in the air for a fatal blow. Suddenly the knight let out a huge, dark shriek, and dropped Luis, to the rocky floor. A huge electric charge emanated from his body, his metal armor conducting the blast, increased the voltage. He shuddered with the force, and his armored plates fell off.

'Now's your chance!' yelled Marina.

Luis leapt up, and slashed the knight's body with his sword, and he started to vaporize.

'Take solace in the light while you can,' cried the knight in a dark tone.

His vaporous body blew into the air, and joined the shadows covering the sky. The rocky caves started to break, and Núria reared her head from the water.

'We must leave, whatever evil you just battled with has

damaged these rocks. Our lives will be at risk if we stay,' said Núria.

Luis helped Marina to her feet, and they grabbed on to Núria's tail, as she swam out of the cave, escaping just before it crumbled. They jumped back into the boat, and Núria quickly brought them back to the shore.

'Thanks for saving us,' said Marina.

'You were the ones who broke the dark curse that had possessed me. Thus I am forever indebted to you,' said Núria. 'But I must ask, why are two youngsters putting themselves in such menacing situations?'

'I need to get home, and the only way I can, is to rid Adastra of this darkness, and restore the moon,' said Luis.

'The shadow has been emanating from Keplar Castle so we set out on this journey to find the King,' added Marina.

'That is very commendable, and I admire your noble hearts. You must believe you can make a change, and change will happen. But be warned…the King may not share such fondness with your actions.'

'What do you know about the King? ' asked Marina.

Núria looked up toward the sky.

'Some time ago something mysterious transpired in the castle, it was a incident which involved the King's children…I wish I knew more for you, but that's all the information I have. If you can meet with someone who knows the royal family then maybe they could reveal more.'

'We know of someone called Mr Plato. He lives on Emerald Bay Island where we wish to travel to next,' said Marina.

'Then you must seek him out, he will be the one to explain this dark mystery. However you must remain careful, swimming in the dark water nearly cost me my life, which is why I was acting so strangely under the water's surface.'

Luis in his thoughts realized why he had so much trouble accessing the Island.

'So it was you that disrupted my compass and our path to the Island,' said Luis.

'Yes, although I wasn't in control of my actions,' said Núria regretfully.

She looked at the two of them curiously.

'But how do you plan on reaching the castle? There is no wind to push you in that direction, nor is the dark water safe to travel.'

Luis produced the half-moon medal and clipped it on to the chain around his neck.

Núria looked at the rare relic in disbelief.

'It can't be?' she gasped.

A familiar rumble echoed throughout the Island, and the cracks on the moon shrunk, lighting more of the land. A fierce wind blew through the air, opening the path toward Emerald Bay Island.

'So the legends are true,' hailed Núria, as she looked to the sky in astonishment.

'I must warn you though, Emerald Bay Island is connected to Keplar Castle by a bridge. That means out of all the four isles, it will be the most dangerous, as the dark powers will be at their peak.'

Marina hearing this information began to worry.

'But don't worry, you two will be fine. What I hate is ignorance, no imagination, and eyes that see no further than their own lashes. You both have extraordinary spirit, and courage. You know what you want, and you've set out to get it. When you doubt yourself you swim against the current of life, but when you trust in yourself, and swim with the current, all things are possible!'

Núria's wisdom filled them with vigor, and they thanked her one last time.

'As you sail away from Sparkling Coral Island, look back in the wind, and I'll show you how the isle got its name,' said Núria cheerfully.

They said their goodbyes and sailed off. From the distance they turned back to see the beautiful array of lights, and watched as Núria using her powers, lit up the small metropolis.

CHAPTER FIVE

The Knight's Sky

"If the stars should appear but one night every
thousands of years how man would marvel and stare"

- Ralph Waldo Emerson

Their voyage was coming to an end, and as the boat
approached Emerald Bay Island Luis noticed an
abundance of tall cliffs surrounding them. This part of
land was completely different from the regions near
Oasis Island, the sea was more rough, and the course
was remarkably treacherous. He got the impression
only skilled sailors would venture this far out. Marina
who had fallen asleep, woke up and rubbed her eyes.
'You were dreaming,' said Luis.
'No I wasn't, I was only down for about ten minutes.'
'Ten minutes? You've been asleep for over an hour!'
Marina started laughing.
'I did dream as a matter of fact. I dreamt that I had

visited your world.'

Luis looked at her, surprised.

'Do you think I would like it? Your world?'

'I think you would. Here in Adastra you only have one ocean, but back home we have several. There all filled with animals, and different types of creatures. But there's no giant talking eels so you might have some trouble getting used to it,' joked Luis.

Marina laughed and looked out toward the sea.

'Can I ask you something Marina?'

'Yeah.'

'Back on Oasis Island, you said your shadows were stolen. Do you still remember the night it happened?'

Marina exhaled, and stared at the sea.

'It happened on the night my father came home, with news that the King had gone missing. At around midnight there was a huge, cracking noise in the sky, and the sound shook everyone's ears. We went outside to check, and looked on in dismay, as the moon started to break in front of our eyes. Then out of nowhere, this weird shadow seeped out from the moons cracks and covered the sky. Days later everyone began to feel weak, and then we realized our shadow had been taken from us, but no one knows why.'

Luis looked at her in a sorrowful manner. But his face suddenly turned to fright.

'Well we might find out sooner than you think!' he

yelled.

She tried to see what he was looking at, but couldn't see anything.

'Marina, crouch down underneath the boat, cover your mouth with your shirt, and don't get up and until I say so.'

She followed his instructions and held her seat tight.

Luis jumped down, and stood in front of her, like a barrier. A huge cloud of dark fog travelled through the air, and surrounded the boat. Luis crouched and covered his nose and mouth with his T-shirt, and held on to Marina, and the pair waited until the fumes blew away.

'We can't let our guard down anymore,' said Luis gasping for air.

'Yeah, we're going to have to be more careful next time,' said Marina.

'At least one thing is for sure,' said Luis, as he went back to the ship's rudder.

'We're close to Keplar Castle, because it looks like Emerald Bay Island is just up ahead.'

The boat got closer and closer, and they noticed the clouds were circling the Island, like a dark halo. As they approached the Island's beach, Marina realized the black fog was getting more thicker.

'Luis change direction! There's a harbor on the other side of the Island. We can try docking there!'

Luis swiftly adjusted the rudder, and veered course, avoiding the haze. They reached the harbor, and there was a lone ship, locked to the dock. Luis tied the boat down, and they jumped on to the small boardwalk. Again the wind blew, and more of the black shadow gusted in their direction. They leapt into the docked ship, and crouched down. Luis noticed it was slightly bigger than their own, and it had a small helm. But the whole boat was dusty, like no one had used it in months. Luis looked over the edge and realized that it was safe to come out, so they crept back on to the boardwalk.

'Wow Núria was right, there's no avoiding the shadow here,' said Luis.

'We're going to have to find some way to completely stop it. Otherwise our whole time on this Island is going to be like one big game of cat and mouse.'

'Well, until we find that last moon medal, we're gonna have to endure,' said Luis.

Marina took out the map and studied it.

'There are two caves on this Island, one near a small village, and the other on top of a cliff.'

'We should kill two birds with one stone, and go to the village. That way we can try and find Mr Plato, and the medal,' said Luis.

*

They tracked through the plains, and after several more encounters with the fog, the pair finally made it to the Island's village. They weren't surprised to find it in an abyss of darkness. There were cobblestoned paths leading to different houses and shops, and all of the windows were bordered up with strong wood. In the center of the village there was a small fountain statue with the royal insignia engraved on it, but the water spewing out was inky black. The aesthetic appeal of this once thriving market town had been absolutely obliterated. The only thing that looked intact was a windmill which sat at the foot of a huge cliff. But it was completely still.

'This is awful,' said Luis.

'Emerald Bay is known to some as the capital Island of Adastra. The last time I visited it was bustling with people of all ages. Now it just looks hideous,' said Marina.

She pulled out the map and tried to stay focused on their mission.

'According to this, there's a cave at the foot of that huge cliff, so we should head there first, then find Mr Plato.'

They ran through the eerie village and dodged the fog simultaneously. The cliff cave was meters away, and Luis whispered Uncle Bruno's ancestor story to psyche himself up. Marina watched him quietly, and wondered what he was saying to himself. He drew his blade with force, and held Marina to the wall.

'Marina stay here and hide, we all know what's lurking in the cave, but this time I'll be ready for the knight when it appears.'

'Wait I'll come with you,' pleaded Marina.

'No it's too dangerous, wait here and watch out for the darkness.'

Luis ran into the cave, and Marina watched him disappear into the small black hole. Minutes passed and Marina started to get worried. Coming out from her hiding spot, she approached the cave. She put one foot into the darkness, and suddenly something grabbed her!

'What are you doing here?'

Marina looked up in fright, but it was just Luis coming out of the cave.

'I told you to hide. If you get hurt Marina that's more blood on my hands, and I can't let that happen.'

'I'm sorry...I got worried.'

'It's okay, to be honest I was worried about you as well, next time just stay close behind me.'

'That sounds like a plan.'

Luis walked back out the cave, and Marina caught up with him.

'Wait! What about the moon medal?'

'There's nothing in there, it just leads to a dead end.'

'So do you think someone took the medal?'

'It's possible, but I think the medal is in the second cave…the one all the way up there.'

Luis looked up at the tall cliff top.

'It hurts my neck just having to even look up so high,' said Marina.

They walked toward the cliff base, and spotted a winding path leading to the top. There was a small gate with a signpost that read.

KEPLAR CASTLE TRAIL

Marina unlocked the gate, but Luis held her shoulder.

She curiously looked up and gasped.

'I hate to say it, but we're going to have to use a different route,' said Luis.

The entire trail was smothered in the jet black fog.

'Is there another way up?' asked Luis.

Marina looked at the map, and shook her head.

'There's no way we can take that path, the fog is blinding. One wrong foot and we'd fall, and if we inhale some of it we might pass out…we're no use to the people of Adastra if we're dead,' said Luis.

'What are we gonna do? How are we supposed to get up there? asked Marina.

'We have to find Mr Plato, he's lived on the Island for

years, maybe he knows if there's an alternate route.'
Marina looked around at the multitude of shops and houses in front of them.

'Time isn't on our side. We're going to have to split up if we want to do this quickly. You take all the houses on the right, and I'll do the left. We'll meet at the center point fountain in ten minutes.'

'Okay let's go,' said Luis.

They hugged each other and ran off in their respective directions. Luis walked to the first house on his right. It was pebble-dashed, and the windows were barricaded with strong wood. He went to knock on the door, but quickly realized it was already open. Inside was a family of five, sitting around a dinner table. Their backs were facing him so he walked up closer.

'Excuse me, I was wondering if you could help me?'
He got closer. Still no response.

'Do you know another way up to Keplar Castle?'
Luis walked up to the table, and approached what looked like the father of the family. His movements made the man spill his wine glass over, but no one attempted to clean up the mess. He looked a little closer and in shock horror realized none of the family were conscious. He grabbed the man's hand, but dropped it immediately as it was ice cold. All of their faces had frightening dark patches under their eyes. Luis shocked, ran out. He checked all the other houses,

but it was the same result. Men, women, and children all unconscious. Scared, he ran to the center fountain to meet Marina, and found her curled up head in hands. As he got nearer, she started to cough violently.

'Marina, are you alright?'

'Everyone's gone...'

'So you've seen it as well?'

'Luis some of these people are my friends!'

He grabbed her hand and realized it was colder than usual.

'Come on, we have to keep looking,' said Luis.

'Looking? Luis Mr Plato is probably gone! It's too late,' she cried.

He hated the thought, but didn't have time to mull it over. He turned to his left and saw the relentless fog hunting them yet again.

'Marina we have to get you inside quick!'

Running away with Marina in hand, he entered a small house on the north west of the village, a few paces opposite the windmill. The house was dead empty, and everything was full of cobwebs. There was an old bookcase near the wall that was hoarding a collection of dusty books. Luis pulled a chair out for Marina. She sat down and started coughing.

'You can't go out there anymore. You're going to have to stay here.'

'I'm fine,' she said, repeatedly sniffing.

'All this close exposure isn't going to do you any good,
I'll find another way to get to the cave,' said Luis.
'What about Mr Plato?'
'For all we know he could be in Keplar Castle, everyone
said he used to work for the King, maybe he's there.'
Luis knelt down and felt Marina's hands.
'See you're warming up slightly, that's why you need to
stay here and recover for a while.'
Luis got up and walked around the room.
'I need to find some way to get up that cliff, and avoid
the darkness at the same time.'
He looked out the window and thought of an idea.
'Marina...I think I just found a way how we can both
get up that cliff safely.'
'How?'
'The windmill,' said Luis confidently. 'Think about it!
Instead of avoiding the darkness, we just blow it all
away!'
'That might actually work,' said Marina optimistically.
'It's not too much of a distance from the house, I could
run there, get in, operate the fans and be back here in
no time.'
'Okay, but hurry back!'
Luis walked to the door.
'I will. Marina stay here, I promise I won't be long.'
As he left, Marina got up to watch from the window,
but the gusting black fog engulfed her view

momentarily. Outside the windmill Luis admired the huge blades, and walked toward the door. He turned the handle. It was locked. Luis thrust his shoulder to the door, but it wouldn't budge. He took some deep breaths in to try and lose the lump in his throat, but in his mind he couldn't help but think that they had fallen at the last hurdle. Back outside the house, he remembered the story of the eagle and he thought of telling it to Marina to lift her spirits, but when he opened the door Marina was gone. Luis froze in disbelief, and then frantically looked everywhere. Under the table, in the kitchen, even breaking down the door to the next house and searching - but she was nowhere to be found. Back in the dark house his knees started to give way, and he sat on the chair where he last left her. His hands were shaking and he started to have flashbacks of Raul hurt. His body out of energy, he slid down the chair, and his kneecaps touched the dusty floor. The silent atmosphere accentuated his thoughts of loneliness, and his eyes leaked with pain. The whole incident was strikingly similar to his moment on the boat where he couldn't find his room, but now he couldn't find Marina. A silent wind hit his wet cheeks and he opened his eyes, wondering where it was coming from. In front of him was a book that had fallen from the bookshelf. It wasn't there before, and he knew he didn't knock it over in his search for Marina. He got up to inspect the bookcase, and found a black hole where the book had been. Reaching through, he found a lever and pulled it. The bookcase opened like a door, and revealed a small flight of steps leading down. He walked down the steps slowly, and then through a dark hallway. He called Marina's name and his voice echoed off the walls, there was a flickering light at the end, and he could feel the promise of warmth. He heard whispering, quietly drew his blade, and leapt out from behind the wall. Marina was there, sitting next to an old man.

'Get away from her now!' yelled Luis.

Marina turned her head and looked at him.

'Luis. This is Mr Plato.'

Mr Plato turned around, and under the dim candlelight Luis looked at his face. He was an old man with grey hair, his skin was etched with wrinkles, and he wore small circular reading glasses. But unlike most people that had been exposed to the darkness, his eyes didn't have dark circles around them. Luis put the blade away and shook his hand. It wasn't cold. But, there was something off-putting about his gaze. His blue eyes were pensive, and he seemed lost, like over time a melancholy had washed over him, eroding his thoughts.

'Nice to meet you,' said Luis.

'Yes, Marina here has told me all about your journey, and your courage in capturing the moon relics.'

Luis nodded his head, his gut feeling about Mr Plato wasn't positive, and he wanted to move things along quickly.

'We were hoping you could help? Everyone that we've met, has said you could give us some information on the King?'

'Well it depends what you've heard…what have you heard?

'Just that you were one of the King's servants and...' Mr Plato interjected.

'One of the King's servants, you heard wrong my boy! I was, and still am in the upper echelons of the Royal service of Adastra.'

'Well then why are you hiding in a secret basement?' said Luis sarcastically.

Marina looked at Luis angrily.

'Now now my boy, times change and we all have to adapt to the environment...I'm curious, as to who's told you what about me?'

'My father, and uncle, told us to speak with you,' said Marina.

'What do they know, about me?' said Mr Plato sternly.

'Just that they spoke with you shortly after all this evil befell Adastra.'

'Is that it?'

'We also spoke to Núria,' said Luis.

'Núria...you spoke with Núria? I'm surprised she's still

alive.'

Luis flashed Marina a concerned look.

'What do you mean by that?' said Luis.

'Nothing! No malice of course, just I'm happy for her, I've probably known Núria longer than both your ages combined,' said Mr Plato.

He walked around the room, struck a match, and lit some candles. There was a candle on the far side of the table, and as Mr Plato stretched and lit it, Luis noticed he was wearing a small golden chain, but he couldn't see its centerpiece. He blew out the match, glanced at Luis's moon chain, and walked toward the lone window. A silhouette of his shadow appeared on the wall opposite as he stared out.

'You know for months I've been watching the world go by, or should I say watching the darkness go by. Then in the last recent hours, I've watched the moon slowly recover, and the sound of the tide come back…I started to think my mind was playing tricks on me, and then when two kids from Oasis Island showed up, I thought I'd truly lost the plot.'

Luis, growing tired of his weird ramblings spoke up.

'Mr Plato we were told that you could help us. Apparently you know what happened to the King?'

'Well you've heard wrong! You've wasted your time coming up here, I'm sorry but I know nothing.'

Marina got up from her chair and stood near Luis.

'Mr Plato, my father and uncle said they...'

'Your father the washed up fisherman, and your uncle the declined knight, know nothing!'

'Núria told us you know something, that it might have something to do with the King's children, the prince and princess of Adastra?' said Luis.

'What did you say?' shrieked Mr Plato.

He started violently shaking and reached in his pocket.

Luis dragged Marina behind his arm, and readied his hand on his blade.

'Don't ever say those words again, get out, get out now!' screamed Mr Plato.

He continued to shake and look out the window. They couldn't see his face but Marina spotted Mr Plato's shadow on the wall, and she knew something was up.

'How has he still got a shadow?' whispered Marina.

'I know you're hiding something Plato. We're not going anywhere until you tell us what you know!' demanded Luis.

He drew his blade, making sure not to make a sound and crept up behind him. He was still shaking rapidly, Luis holding the blade tight, swerved round to get a glimpse of his face. Once he did he was shocked at what he saw.

'Marina give me that chair quick!' shouted Luis.

Mr Plato suddenly fell backward, but Luis cushioned his fall, and sat him down in the chair. He took off his glasses and the salt of his soul leaked from his eyes, each translucent trickle adding to his grief.

'It's my fault,' yelled Mr Plato. 'I'm so sorry!'

Luis put away his weapon, and Marina found a cloth on the table and gave it to him. Mr Plato dabbed away his tears.

'I haven't been completely honest with you, or with anyone for that matter.'

'So you do know what happened?' examined Luis.

'Yes, it was an accident, a horrible accident.'

Marina looked at Luis shocked. Both of them eager to hear what Mr Plato had to say.

'One day when the King was busy he told me to look after his son and daughter. The prince and princess of Adastra. I used to love taking them fishing. So we took my boat and sailed out far. It was a peaceful evening, and the Sea of Serenity's gentle waves danced in the singing wind. Time passed and we caught a number of fish. They wanted to go back home and show their father their catches, so we set sail back to the castle. Sensing the possibility of a storm, I sailed as fast as I could. But the clouds in the sky turned ominously dark, and rain pelted the boat. Then the sound of thunder broke the sky, and the songs from the wind turned into screams. The boat couldn't handle the torment, and I lost control. Water poured in from all angles, and the waves relentlessly licked the boat as if it wanted to taste our deaths. I gave up steering, and just cradled the two children. Eventually the boat capsized, and we were stranded. I survived, and washed up on Emerald Bay isle, but the children weren't so fortunate. To this day, I still can't forget the sound of their cries.'

Mr Plato wiped away the last of his tears.

'I'm so sorry,' said Luis.

'So what happened when you told the King?' asked Marina.

'The King kept the whole story bottled up, and only told his trusted knights. A huge search party was sent out to try and find them, but the only thing they found was my damaged boat. Over time the King's sympathy turned into hatred. He knew the whole thing was an accident, but he blamed me for their deaths.'

'Is that why Marina's uncle said he heard the two of you arguing?'

'We had many heated discussions, so there was a high chance your Uncle Bruno was present.'

'So what happened to the King?' asked Luis.

'He drifted into a state of madness, banning people from the castle, even his workers from the Island. He was alone, upset that no one could carry on the royal bloodline, and heir his throne. Months passed and his mind started to atrophy. I had to start telling people that the King had gone missing. I didn't want the people of Adastra thinking the King had gone mad.

More time passed and things took a evil twist. Every night he would go out to his balcony and curse the full moon for doing this to his children. He wished for something to take him away. Then as time passed, his dark wish came true. He came down with a severe depression and sickness, losing his will to live, and he gave in to the darkness. Soon this dark entity appeared, and usurped his throne. Keplar Castle is now the stronghold for who you can call, The Shadow King.'

Marina and Luis both looked at each other stunned, they had finally discovered the real reason behind all the mysterious goings on.

'So this Shadow King, I understand he's the person behind all of this but if it's just the King deep down can't he be talked out of it?' asked Luis.

'You don't understand, the real King, just like everyone on this forsaken Island is gone. If something isn't done soon, everyone will be consumed.'

'So how come you still have your shadow, why weren't you affected? asked Luis.

'Because I've been in hiding for months. Not even the Shadow King or his knights know where I am.'

Marina consoled Mr Plato, and he looked at Luis's moon medal as it dangled from his neck.

'You must finish your mission and procure that last relic to form the moon medallion. It is our only chance of dethroning the King, and ridding Adastra of this evil.'

'That was our plan, but we can't get up that hill, because of the fog barrier, and we're pretty sure the last relic is located in the cave up there. We tried to power the windmill, to blow away the darkness, but the door is locked shut,' said Luis.

'I think I can be of some assistance then,' said Mr Plato. He reached into his shirt and pulled out the chain from around his neck.

'This is key for the windmill, use it as you please.'

Mr Plato handed Luis the key. A smile appeared on his face and he let out a small laugh.

'I don't believe it!' said Luis, and he looked at Marina. 'We can finally get that last medal!'

'You must be careful though. The Shadow King turned three of his best knights into his dark minions and made them guard the relics.'

'So that's why every time I've defeated them they materialize, they're part of the Kings curse?'

'Yes, he knew of their ancient power, and that if anyone dared assemble them, his dark days would be over. Restore the moon, and you destroy the King.'

Luis went to the exit.

'Thank you Mr Plato, you really are a strong man. Their death was not your fault, and where ever they are now, I'm sure they know how much you loved and cared for them.'

'Thank you Luis.'

Luis left, but heard footsteps catching up to him.

'I'm coming with you.' said Marina. 'I feel much better now. We've gone on this journey together and we'll finish it together.'

Luis smiled at her, and knew she wouldn't take no for an answer. Marina thanked Mr Plato, and followed Luis back out to the village.

*

Outside the windmill, Luis unlocked the door and stepped inside. There was a coiling wooden staircase that spiraled to the top. He climbed the stairs and rotated the lever, and the huge bladed fans started to turn. He ran back outside to join Marina, and together they watched, as the dark clouds were blown away by the powerful generated wind. The Keplar Castle cliff trail was finally safe to travel.

*

Luis and Marina were almost at the top of the cliff. It was a winding trail, that led all the way up to the five hundred foot high summit. The ground was rocky, and every so often Luis had to take off his shoes, to remove the small stones that had fallen in.

'I can't stop thinking about Mr Plato's story,' said Marina. 'It's just so heart-breaking.'

'I know…the only thing we can do, is try our best to return Adastra to its old self, and hopefully this evil King will disappear.'

Luis taking his mind off the matter, watched as a small stream trickled down the cliff. They were incredibly high up and he could see the water flowing all the way down to the harbor.

'So how did Emerald Bay Island get its name Marina?'

'Years ago this Island was a founding place for many of the jewels and emeralds that would be worn by the royal family. I would always cherish the time spent on this Island. It's the oldest Island in Adastra, so coming here is like being a part of history.'

Before Luis responded, Marina interrupted him.

'Luis can I ask you something?'

'Yeah go ahead.'

'Why do you keep whispering to yourself every time you're near something dangerous?'

Luis stopped and looked back at her, almost as if he was annoyed.

'I haven't been spying on you or anything, it's just back in the Sparkling Coral cave you were reciting something, and you did it again before the cave in the village. If it's personal, I understand if you don't want to talk about it.'

'Personal?' Luis let out a small laugh. 'No, I've just been going over a story your Uncle Bruno told me.'

'It wasn't one of his knight tales was it?'

'No, after the whole Raul incident he could see I was shaken up, so he told me a story about how I have the blood of warriors and champions. When I first heard it, I was so inspired. But when I was squaring off with the knight, the inspiration was gone.'

They carried on trudging up the hill, and Marina spoke up from behind.

'You know Luis, I remember when I was a little girl my father would tell me stories of the ocean, and I would get so excited, but one thing I'll never forget is my first day sailing. I was so scared, and I questioned my love for the sea, but he kept taking me, and after time my fears faded, and my love for the sea grew. It taught me that nothing in the world can substitute experience. You can read quotes, and hear inspiring stories, but being out there every day will change you from the core.'

Marina slipped, but Luis grabbed her hand and pulled her back up.

'Yeah you're right, and that can only be done through trial and error,' said Luis.

He knew exactly what she meant, and thought about everything she'd said as he walked to the cliff top. Reaching the end, they climbed up some rocky steps, and onto the flat summit. The first thing Luis saw was the gigantic Keplar Castle sitting atop a distant cliff. Its imposing dark grey structure blended with the black sky. There were three stone pillars, each with black pointed roofs, and tall stained glass windows. In the middle, was a towering steeple pillar, emitting the deadly nocturnal smog. Its current appearance, reflected the evil prestige and power of its current occupant.

'There it is, Keplar Castle,' said Luis.

'This is horrible, I remember when it used to look like a castle from a fairy-tale. Now it just looks like factory for pollution. Luis we have to get that last medal, I can't take much more of this,' cried Marina.

Luis scanned the area, to spot the cave. There were a few trees at the edge of the cliff, and he walked toward them to investigate. Behind them was a narrow sloping path leading toward a rocky hole.

'I haven't forgotten our deal Marina. Follow in close behind me.'

'Okay, I'll be on the lookout for the knight as well.'

He drew the blade, crouched under the rocks, and entered the hole. The last small silver box sat inside. The space was incredibly small, and there was nowhere the knight could materialize from. Luis crept down and blew the orange rocky dust off the box, and unclipped the lock, but there was nothing inside. Suddenly Luis thought of Marina. Where has she gone? Luis crept out of the cave immediately, and heard the sound of dragging feet. He followed the path back to the summit and saw the knight wearing the final moon chain, his sword pressed on Marina's soft neck. The knight waved the medal in front of him.

'You're too late!' he rasped.

'Luis I'm sorry! He grabbed me the second you went in the cave.'

The knight eyed Luis's chain.

'How about we make a trade? You throw me the chain around your neck, and I throw you the girl?'

Luis looked at the chain on his neck.

'No! Luis don't, it took us so long to acquire those relics. If you give them to him, he'll destroy them!' yelled Marina.

'The girl clearly has a death wish! Don't be so foolish!' shrieked the knight.

Luis drew the blade.

'Stop hiding behind "a girl." You win, you get the medal, and some of your pride back,' taunted Luis.

The knight loosened some of his grip on Marina, and Luis carried on tempting him.

'What would the King say? If he knew one of his former warriors had to use a little girl as shield?'

The knight savagely tossed Marina to the side, and she quickly crawled behind Luis. The knight wore its silver armor, and like the others his face was hidden by a metal visor. This knight in particular, was wielding a sword and a black spiked shield. The moonlight shone down onto the cliff top arena, and the knight charged at Luis like a bull. Luis retreating parried his blows with his sword. In the corner of his eye he saw Marina, and remembered her wise words about experience. With so much was at stake, he couldn't keep defending, it was time to attack. Luis powerfully swung his sword, the knight not expecting it quickly covered his face with his shield. Luis crouched down and scooped up some of the rocky dust on the ground. He waited until the knight lowered his shield, and threw the dust into the knight's helmet, seeping through the gaps in his visor, and blotting his vision. The knight dropped his sword and shield, and attended to his helmet. Luis, sensing his chance, pushed him to the cliff's edge, raised his weapon and with the very tip of the blade lifted the chain from around the knight's neck. The knight cleared his vision, but it was too late! Luis raised the sword and slashed him, he fell off the edge, and Luis watched as he hurtled down, and crashed into the sea.

'You did it,' said Marina.

Luis opened his clenched fist and stared at the last moon medal. It was finally over. They heard a noise from behind, and the pair looked over quickly.

It was just Mr Plato.

'What are you doing here?' shouted Luis happily.

'I got slightly worried, and decided to come up, in case you were hurt.'

Luis lifted up the moon medal chain, showing it to him.

'Well now I'm glad I joined you, how could I miss a moment like this,' added Mr Plato.

They walked to the center of the cliff and stared at the moon.

'You ready?' asked Luis.

They looked on eagerly at the moon and sky. Luis took the final medal, the shape of a left crescent moon, and clipped it on to the chain. Completing the pendant and forming the full moon medallion. A thunderous roar echoed from below the sea bed. The cliff shook violently, and the three of them all held on to each other. Small parts of the moon broke off and crumbled into the sea, and slowly the black fissures straightened up and vanished. The full moon had returned, and its stunning luminescent light shone over Adastra. Luis and Marina jumped for joy and hugged one another.

'Luis you can finally go home! Thank you!' exclaimed Marina. They celebrated and shouted, but the pair hadn't noticed something. Mr Plato was silent, and he wasn't smiling. He stared out toward the sea, and turned toward Keplar Castle.

'Luis you're not going anywhere,' said Mr Plato.

Luis and Marina turned to see what Mr Plato was

looking at, and their smiles vanished. The dark clouds enveloping Keplar Castle were still there, and the smog was still pouring out from its rooftop.

'The moon might be restored, but where are the stars? That shadow is still emanating from the castle and destroying the land,' said Mr Plato.

'I thought you said assembling the moon medallion would restore the moon and get rid of the darkness?'

'Yes, but unfortunately I overlooked one thing, it didn't get rid of the Shadow King. As long as he still sits on the throne, that toxic cloud is going to destroy everyone. The only way for Adastra to return to normal, and for you to return home, is to defeat the King,' said Mr Plato.

'Luis I'm so sorry,' said Marina 'I thought...'

'No don't be sorry, we have to finish this. We have to destroy him,' said Luis.

'You're going to go after the Shadow King?' asked Mr Plato.

'We've defeated all of his knights, how tough can he be?' said Luis.

Mr Plato looked at him, maybe Luis was right, he thought. The trio walked toward the edge of the cliff. A long wooden bridge, suspended high in the air connected the two cliff tops. Five hundred feet beneath them was the Sea of Serenity. They walked along, but halfway across Marina stopped.

'Marina what are you doing? We don't have time to take a break,' said Luis.

She remained silent and Luis tracked back to see what she was staring at.

'Look up at the tower,' said Marina.

Luis looked up and noticed the shadows from the center steeple had stopped emitting. Suddenly something started to materialize in front of them. Small shadow clusters grouped together and formed into the shape of a human. Then a dark fog engulfed the bridge, and blinded the three of them. It slowly evaporated, and standing in front of them under the pale moonlight, was none other than the Shadow King. He was tall and menacing, and carried with him an aura of cruelty. His face was covered in a huge spiked metal helmet, and there were two small holes for his eyes. There was a visor in front of his mouth, and his dark gaseous body was protected in the King's armor, but he had decorated it with darkness - black spiked metal plaques on his shoulders, forearms, and hands. Slowly, a pair of crimson red eyes opened and glared at the three of them.

'Bow down to the King!' he snarled in a vitriolic tone.

Luis and Marina trembled, but Mr Plato slowly stood in front of him, and knelt down. The Shadow King produced a heavy black sword, the tip was curved like an axe.

'Mr Plato you've evaded my dark grasp for far too long. But you've finally decided to show yourself. I must thank you for your bravery.'

He put the flat side of the blade on Mr Plato's shoulder, as if to knight him. Mr Plato clamped his eyes shut, and apologized to him. Wasting no time, the Shadow King raised his sword and viciously swiped him. A loud metallic noise rumbled the air, and Mr Plato hit the bridge wall with terminal impact. Breathing heavily in pain, he stretched his hand out for Luis and Marina to grab.

'You should have stayed in hiding. You can blame the two of them for your demise.'

The Shadow King kicked him out of his path, and walked forward toward Luis.

'When you meet a swordsman, draw your sword!' rasped the King.

Luis slowly drew his blade, and looked up at the moon.

He held the blade up and reflected some of the moonlight onto the Shadow King's face, but nothing happened. The Shadow King started laughing to himself.

'I admire your feeble attempts boy. Silly tricks like that might work on my knights, or that stupid cursed eel, but they won't work on the King.'

He turned to Marina.

'The fisherman's daughter, and the niece to one my

former knights. I'm guessing this pathetic idea of restoring the moon was yours? I must admit, I am surprised at the lengths you've gone to, but you've wasted your time.'

Luis had enough. He charged with the blade and struck him, but the King grabbed it with his hands. Black cracks proliferated its shiny surface and seeped down toward the hilt. Luis let go and shrieked in pain, he grabbed his hand and tried to rid the weird burning sensation. Luis looked up as he threw his blade down to the floor. Mr Plato still in severe pain sensed Luis was in danger and crawled in front of him.

The Shadow King looked down on him in disgust.

'There's no use taking your shadow, it will only make me weaker.' He quickly turned to Luis.

'But you, you must be punished!'

He outstretched the palm of his hand, raised it above Luis's head, and let out a horrifying roar. Marina screamed for him to stop. Luis dropped to his knees, as if something had just drained his energy. Marina looked down on the bridge floor and watched as his shadow disappeared.

'Now that I have your shadow, you can never leave this place, and just to make sure of it...'

The Shadow King moved his hand to the side, and from the vantage point of the bridge, spotted their sailboat in the harbor. He shot a huge dark sphere toward it, shattering it to pieces.

'In a few hours darkness will eclipse all of Adastra.
If you want to survive a few hours more I'd suggest you leave now, and get a head start back to Oasis Island.'

He pointed to Mr Plato, 'And take him with you!'

The Shadow King let out a huge evil laugh, and he started to materialize into the darkness.

'Adastra is mine...' and he vanished.

Luis got up slowly, and a huge shadow started to envelop the bridge.

'We have to get off this bridge now!' yelled Marina.

Luis grabbed Mr Plato and covered him with his cape, shielding him from the noxious fumes.

Back on the cliff they laid Mr Plato down on the floor, and watched as the huge shadow covered the entire bridge, blocking the entry to Keplar Castle. Mr Plato started to cough excruciatingly, and he pointed his finger at Luis.

'Luis he's dying we have to do something quick!' cried Marina.

'Wait, I think he's trying to tell me something,' said Luis.

He knelt down beside him.

'What is it? Mr Plato please tell me?'

He took his hand and grabbed Luis's cape, pinching it with his shaking hand.

'Luis he wants your cape, give it to him!'

Mr Plato shook his head, and grabbed the cape tight in his clenched fist.

'Where...did you get this from?' coughed Mr Plato.

'The cape? Marina's father gave it to me.'

'It's not possible, this cape...it belongs to the prince.'

Mr Plato looked at the stitching on the cape's underside and confirmed it. Luis looked up at Marina in awe.

'There's nothing you can do to save me...I can feel my body materialising as we speak, but this discovery has given me renewed hope...I can't believe I didn't spot it sooner. The cape you're wearing is known as the Luna Cape. It is said that whoever wears it, combined with the moon medallion, will grant the user similar powers to the moon. But no one has ever seen it to believe it.'

He started coughing again, and held his hand over his heart.

'Luis, Marina...if you want to defeat the Shadow King you must do one last thing. You must revive Luis's broken blade, and infuse it with the moonlight...then it will be able to cut through the Kings dark armor. There is a place in Adastra, the same place I used to take the prince and princess fishing. It is a sacred hidden Island, that not even the King knows about...it houses the highest point in all of Adastra, where you'll be closest to the moon. Go there and hold the blade into the moonlight.'

'But how can we get there? We don't have a boat.' said

Marina.

'Go back to the house, there is a book on the top right of the shelf, it will explain everything. Open it and take what is there. Hurry, there isn't much time left. The more shadows the king consumes, and the longer the darkness lingers, the more he will keep growing in power. You must defeat him soon! Only then will Adastra return to normal.'

Luis and Marina thanked him, but before he could wish them well, he vaporized into the darkness.

CHAPTER SIX

Dethroning The King

"Everyone is a moon, and has a dark side to which
   he never shows to anybody"

- Mark Twain

Luis and Marina sprinted back down from the trail and
entered Mr Plato's house. Marina clambered up onto
the bookcase, and grabbed the book.
'Are you sure that's the right one?' asked Luis.
'It has to be, he did say on the very far right.'
Marina shook the book and heard something inside.
She jumped down and put it on the table. The first
couple of pages had been cut out, and there was a small
square hole containing a small key.
'I wonder what it's for?' asked Marina.
She flicked through the book, and noticed some of the
pages had been ripped out, but the last few pages were
adorned with handwriting.
'It looks like some sort of diary,' examined Marina, and
she started reading.

February 1st,

Today I've got permission from the king to take the prince and princess out. The weather has been terrific lately so I'm going to take them to Mount Moon Cove. I can see why the mysterious spot has eluded people in the past, with its treacherous maze entrance.

Right, right, left, right, left, I think that's the path I took!

I've marked the location on my map, but I must memorise the maze sequence for future visits. It's funny how you can stumble upon great things when you're lost at sea...

The last time I took them sailing we had so much fun, the kids really love being out on the ocean. I've got a surprise in store for them today. I've hired some fishing equipment from the harbor. I can't wait to see the looks on their precious faces when they catch some fish.

We've grown so close over the years, and spending time with them has made me realize just how much I love them....Anyway I must go and prepare the boat!

Bon Voyage!

'Wow, he must have written this on the day of the accident,' said Marina.

'Do you think anyone else has read it?' asked Luis.

'I doubt it. There's a lot of negative stigma around Mr Plato in regards to Adastra's situation, he must have kept it guarded.'

Luis walked around the room, and spotted a map of Adastra framed on the wall. It was identical to their map, but with a pin stuck in it.

'Marina look! This must be the location.'

She took out her map and held them together.

'It looks like Mount Moon Cove is just a few miles North West of Keplar Castle.'

Marina shook her head in confusion.

'What do you think the key is for then?'

Luis looked through his diary entry and searched for an answer, suddenly he had a flashback of when he and Marina first landed on the Island.

'That's it! It's the key to his boat, the one we saw in the harbor.'

Marina marked the location of Mount Moon Cove on her map.

'Let's go!' she said quickly.

Back in the harbor, Luis used Mr Plato's key and unlocked the boat. It was more spacious than their last sailboat, and equipped with three sails making it much faster.

'Wow this boat is amazing, we should reach Mount Moon Cove in no time,' said Marina.

Luis adjusted the sails, and went to the helm. He steered the boat out of the harbor, and headed toward the mysterious cove.

*

The boat moved along quickly, aided by the power of the full moon and the tides. Around four miles North West from Keplar Castle, they came across a dead end - full of cliffs.

'According to the map, there's a whole section of land behind these tall rocks,' explained Marina.

Luis spotted a narrow gap in between two tall cliffs and carefully steered the boat through it.

'Do you think many people know of this place?' asked Luis.

'I don't think so. I doubt anyone knows this spot exists. I mean, who would dare sail out this far?'

They entered a valley, and the huge shoulders of the cliff tops made the boat a spec in comparison. Unexpectedly the boat entered a rapid, and the agitated white water rocketed them forward! Marina fell down and dropped the book.

'Hold on Marina!' shouted Luis.

The boat swayed left and right violently, and then out

of nowhere a fork appeared in the pathway. Luis turned to Marina for guidance.

'Marina which way left or right?'

'I don't know it off by heart, the path is written in the book.'

'Marina I need to know now, or we'll crash into that rock!'

As the rapids jolted the boat, Marina crawled to the book and grabbed it. The boat was inches away from the rock.

'Marina which way!?'

Marina flicked through the pages.

'Marina?!'

'Right, go right!'

Luis slammed the wheel and the boat veered right.

Marina instructed Luis with the directions, and he maneuvered the boat out of harm's way. They entered a calm body of water that was surrounded by cliffs, not much wind was finding its way to the sails, and Luis lowered them. In the distance was a huge pyramidal silhouetted rock, so tall it looked like its pointed summit pierced the moon. The narrow ocean path started to bend like a horseshoe, and there was a small sandy beach in front of a tiny cave. Luis steered the boat onto the sand, and they hopped out onto the beach. The water was an intense turquoise, with small ripples of white foam quenching the serene shore. Luis looked down onto its mirrored surface. It reminded him of the pool on the cruise ship.

Marina put her hand in and swooshed the water.

'You know, I think this is the only place in the whole of Adastra that hasn't been intoxicated by the darkness… If the stars were out, I bet they'd be reflecting on the crystal surface,' said Marina.

'Well something tells me Adastra has many beautiful secrets,' added Luis.

He heard the sound of a waterfall, and went through the small cave to the other side. There was a tiny pool of water, with two cascading waterfalls on its left and right. In between were steps leading up to the tall rock. Luis looked up and realized the steps snaked around to the pointed summit. He washed his hands and face in the small pool of water.

'Marina it's a long way to the top, there's no point in both of us getting tired…I'm gonna go it alone.'

'Okay, I understand. I'll wait here for you…good luck!'

The stone steps were wet from the waterfall's splashing mist, so Luis walked slowly. After a few moments, he took a deep breath, and ran up the spiralling steps to the summit of Mount Moon Cove.

*

Luis advanced quickly, despite his bruised knees and

hands cut from slipping. He was only a few steps from the top, and the wind was becoming ever forceful. His legs were cramping, so he sat down to take a break. For the first time in a long time, he thought about his parents. He'd gone through so much and he wished his parents were here to see him. He knew their notions about him weren't strong, and he got frustrated because all of his courage would go un-noticed. Marina was the only one who'd been supporting him, and now she was hundreds of feet below. Time passed, and the mellow light of the moon hit the rock, jolting his train of thought. And he started to realize that hard work is always cultivated when no one's watching - outside of the lime light or in this case the moonlight. Feeling energized, he got up, and ran the final steps to the summit. The little voice in his head kept telling him to quit, but he refused to listen. He sped round the last bend, and leapt the final steps to the summit. The view was entrancing, and he could see all of Adastra. From the small houses of Oasis Island, to the forestation in Aquatic Reef, Sparkling Coral's arresting visuals, and the harbor of Emerald Bay. But his sense of wonderment was cut short as he turned to the left and seen the smog of Keplar Castle. It reminded him of his mission. With that in mind he looked up at the full moon - like a giant pearl in the night sky. He unsheathed the Royal Blade, and held it up. The moonlight purified the blade, and the black cracks on its steel surface melted away. Suddenly the moon flared a white light, and the blade became infused with the moon's luminescent glow.

*

Back in the cove Marina sat by the small pool of water. She found a unique coloured seashell and put it in her pocket. All of a sudden, she heard the sound of footsteps. She looked up toward the rocky steps and saw a small shimmering light bouncing off the walls. She got up and saw Luis slowly walking down the steps, the blades glorious glow forced her to squint her eyes. He held the blade up, and she smiled at him. Luis seemed different with this majestic new look, almost as if his trials and tribulations were starting to affect his beliefs. He jumped down into the sand and walked toward her. Marina even noticed his walk was different, his head was high, and his shoulders no longer slumped. Luis showed her the blade.

'When I held it up in front of the moon, it absorbed the moonlight. So I think we should call it the Luna blade. Now it should be strong enough to cut through the darkness.'

'Wow it looks sublime, I never expected it to glow like that!' expressed Marina.

Luis began walking toward the boat.

'Marina we have to leave now. On the way down, I had a brief encounter with the Shadow King.'

Marina caught up. 'What do you mean!?'

'He knows we're here, and he's covered the whole of Adastra in his dark cloud.'

Luis jumped onto the boat and helped her up.

'So does that mean the darkness has swallowed Oasis Island?' asked Marina.

Luis remained silent.

'My parents are on that Island!'

He put his hand on her shoulder.

'Everyone is gone Marina. It's just me and you. All of this will end once we dethrone the King...I know it's hard to take in, but we haven't got time to sit and sulk.'

Luis raised the sails, and steered the boat out of the cove, back into the white water.

'Get ready to hold on tight Marina!'

Instantly they were assailed by huge clouds of darkness. Luis used the Luna blade to increase his visibility, but it was still difficult to see. All of a sudden they heard the Shadow King's voice.

'Look around you! All of Adastra has been covered in darkness. Your parents, your uncle, your brother, everyone who you're desperately trying to save, their souls belong to me...good luck finding your way back to my castle!'

His bitter laugh trailed off, and Marina looked around trying to see.

'Luis how are we supposed to get out?!' she yelled.

Despite the danger of capsizing, Luis raised the sails and steered the boat forward. In anger, he began swiping at the fog causing it to disappear.

'Luis you can't do that forever! We're sailing at such a high speed, one wrong turn and we'll crash!'

Luis tried to hold the boat still but the water was too powerful.

'Marina I can't stop it!'

As the boat jolted forward in the rapids, a warm wind suddenly gusted through the air, and the dark fog around the boat turned into a blue mist. Luis stood in front of her with the blade. But Marina wasn't scared, she spotted something near the bow, and walked in front of him.

'Marina what are you doing?'

'Luis put your sword away,' she said calmly.

He put the blade back in his scabbard and joined her.

Looking up he saw two small transparent figures drifting above the ship's bow. One of them was an outline of a boy, and the other a small girl. The two figures gently smiled at them, and a soft voice emanated from around the boat.

'Follow us...'

Luis's still in shock slowly walked to the helm.

'We have to hurry,' the voice echoed.

Luis steered the boat into the turbulent water, and the two spirits floated forward, leaving a trail of blue mist.

'Look, they're showing us the way out, stay close behind them!' shouted Marina.

Luis stayed within range, and followed the mist around a sharp right turn and a swooping left. Steering and swiveling around the rocks, he veered the boat around a right curve.

'Hold on,' said the voice.

Marina grabbed onto Luis's arm as the boat pivoted around the cliffs, and sailed out of the white water maze. Luis, now safely behind the two souls, navigated the boat through the narrow gap in the rock, and back onto the calm Sea of Serenity. Luis looked up at the two entities.

'Thank you.'

'Yes, we owe you our lives,' said Marina.

The two spirits looked at each other and smiled.

She looked at the spirit of the young boy.

'You must be the prince?'

'Yes, I am the prince of Adastra, and this is my younger sister.'

Luis couldn't help but feel sad.

'I'm sorry about what happened...to you and your sister.'

'Mr Plato told us everything. He loves you both so

much and he misses you,' added Marina.

'We miss him too...we also miss our father.'

Luis looked at the prince confused. He didn't seem shaken up or regretful by the tragic incidents that had befallen him.

'I don't understand, how can you be so calm?'

'Yes, the incident is upsetting, but you mustn't let anger fill your sad hearts. Look what's happened to Adastra because of our father's repressed anger. He's turned from a loving King to someone who resents all forms of life.'

'Wait, you mean you know what happened to your father?' asked Marina.

'It's hard not to notice what's befell Adastra in these dark times. Which is why our souls at this moment are unrested.'

Luis still hadn't gotten over their death, and was still showing signs of sadness.

'But you were so young, you had so much to live for, aren't you upset?'

There was a brief moment of silence and then the prince spoke up again.

'When me and my sister passed on...yes we were young, but we were happy. Even on the day of our death we were doing something we loved. If up to our deaths we were pursuing something that was against our impulses, then that is what can cause the feeling you know as regret.'

The prince looked at the spirit of his younger sister.

'So young, so beautiful, and happy...you see death has no discriminations, it can strike the rich, the poor, even children. But you mustn't shy away from such a fate. Everything in life is connected, from the moon and the tides, to life and death.'

'But on the day of the accident weren't you afraid?' asked Luis.

'Even the darkest hour has only sixty minutes...Luis you must start to see this as something positive. Strive to do what you love every day, because you never know what might happen...I shouldn't have to explain further, because what you're both doing is a shining example of two people following their deepest desires.'

The prince's spirit slowly started to evaporate.

'We cannot stay for long, but you must finish your quest. Keplar Castle is three miles north...our father is still alive somewhere in the castle. I can feel his energy.'

Marina looked stunned.

'The real King...your father is still alive?'

'Yes, only just...please rid Adastra of this shadow, and tell the King we love him. Then we can finally rest in peace.'

'We'll tell him. I promise,' said Marina.

'Thank you, once again,' said Luis.

'We'll forever be with you...in your hearts and in your

spirits,' said the Prince.

They vanished, and his voice echoed away in the wind.

'I can't believe we actually met the prince and princess of Adastra,' said Marina.

'Yeah, all that bottled sadness I had for them has gone. I feel glad to have met them,' said Luis.

'We have to keep our promise, and repeat the prince's words to the King so they can rest in peace.'

'Well, if we want to tell him, we have to get moving.' Luis walked to the front of the ship.

'Marina, this time I need you to operate the sails and I'll be at the helm. I need to cut away the darkness with the Luna blade.'

Marina lifted the sails and Luis steered the ship toward the castle.

*

As time passed, the darkness around the boat became colossal. They were sailing at top speed and the polluting towers of Keplar Castle were drawing closer. Luis hopped onto the bow and used the blade as a beacon. Marina looked on concerned.

'Luis I know you're doing the best you can, but we're running out of time. Remember we still have to get to Emerald Bay Island, up that cliff, and into the castle. I'm worried we're not going to make it!'

Luis, not wanting to show signs of disbelief, continued to cut away the darkness from the front of the boat. Her words had a bitter truth in them, and he knew in his heart, time wasn't on their side.

'We can still try,' he said defiantly.

The boat approached the cliff supporting Keplar Castle, and Marina scanned the area for hidden pathways, and short-cuts, but she couldn't find anything. She looked up to the castle, the dark clouds still encompassing its roof, and the moon shining directly above its steeple. Luis was standing on the bow using the Luna blade's glowing guidance, and the Luna cape was flapping uncontrollably in the wind. All of a sudden something caught Marina's attention.

'Luis, I think I know how you can reach the castle!'

Luis stopped what he was doing and walked toward her. Marina took a deep breath.

'I know this is going to sound weird, but...use the wind to fly up to the castle!'

Luis looked at her like she had gone mad.

'Do you remember what Mr Plato said? Whoever wears the Luna cape and the full moon medallion will be able to harness the powers of the moon.'

'Yeah I remember, but then he said no one has ever seen it to believe it.'

'Well maybe we have reverse the process...believe it... to see it.'

'What do you mean?'

Marina pointed to the ship's bow.

'Luis, jump from the boat, and believe, really trust in yourself that you can control the wind, and use it to fly to the castle.'

'Are you out of your mind?'

'No I'm not. Luis your beliefs about anything will always shape your reality.'

She sensed that Luis was struggling with the idea.

'Luis look at me.'

Luis stared into her deep hazel eyes.

'I remember when you first arrived on the beach, you were this scared boy with a hidden power inside of you. As we've gone on this adventure your mind has been exposed to new ventures, you've had brushes with death, and your courage has gone from a dwindling flame to a roaring blaze. Look at you now, you're finally at the helm of your life. Now the last thing you have to do is take that leap of faith toward your own noble horizon.'

Luis started having flashbacks of everything he's been through since washing up on Oasis Island. After a brief pause, he realized she was right.

'Okay...I'll do it.'

Marina hugged him and he walked toward the front of the ship, climbing onto the boat's bow. He held his head high and walked up the acute apex. He pulled out the moon medallion from underneath his shirt, and kissed the pendant. He took a deep breath in, and with his eyes open, he walked to the very tip of the bow. He looked up at the full moon that he had restored, then peered down at the black intoxicated water crashing off the boat's body.

The ship was travelling at an immense speed, and with the wind blustering his cape, he leapt off the bow.

Marina ran to the front, but Luis wasn't there. She looked out from the sides and ran to the stern, but she still couldn't see him. Suddenly a huge gale gusted through the air, moving her hair from her eyes, she looked up toward the bow. There was a silhouetted figure floating in front of the moon. As he flew down toward her, a gentle breeze brushed her cheeks.

'You did it! I can't believe you're actually flying!'

'You can't believe it? If it wasn't for you I wouldn't have believed it!'

Marina started laughing at her silly choice of words.

Luis drew the blade and held it by his side.

'Marina I'm going to fly up to the cliff and clear the trail for you. Then I'm going to enter Keplar Castle and dethrone the Shadow King.'

'What about me, what do you want me to do?'

'For now, stay safe. Meet me atop the cliff when the King is gone.'

'But how will I know!?'

'When the King falls the darkness will scatter.'

Marina gave him a warm smile, 'Good luck!'

Luis shut his eyes, and a huge whirlwind appeared underneath him. His cape lifted up with the wind, and he whizzed off in the air current. He flew through Emerald Bay Island, and using the Luna blade's light destroyed the dark fog surrounding the village. He flew up the cliff trail and cleansed the pathway making it safe for Marina to travel. Luis reached the top off the cliff and walked toward the bridge. There was a vortex of darkness obstructing the entrance. He took the blade and plunged it into the hole, breaking the dark seal. The dark haze around the bridge evaporated and Luis walked across. He reached the entrance, dragged the handle of the grand wooden door, and entered Keplar Castle. Luis walked through the foyer. It was eerily spooky, and he looked around the luxurious but lonely space. Minimal moonlight crept through the stained glass windows and shone on the cold marble floor. The sound of his footsteps bounced off the walls filling the silence. To his right, he spotted a large library, and walking through he noticed the walls were covered in prestigious portraits of the castles former ancestors.

At the end he reached two towering marble columns leading to another room. The ceilings in this room were covered in a beautifully woven tapestry, accentuating the castle's renaissance feel. A soft red carpet cushioned his feet, and he followed it to find a small double staircase, leading to another spiraling set of stairs. A small sign read:

"Stairs leading to Throne Room"

After a long ascent, he reached the top, and found a long narrow hallway. The windows were open and the breeze pushed the red curtains up and down. The walls were covered in weaponry and there were knight statues scattered around evenly. Each one reminded him of his significant battles on each Island. Finally, he reached a grand wooden door, and opened it into the throne room. The room was huge, with a long red carpet leading up to the high-back throne. Walking toward it he noticed it had a marble finish, and was planted on a on a five-step raised platform which augmented its powerful prestige. Behind the throne were two outstretched window-doors leading out to a balcony. Despite their height the black fog pressed against the plate glass windows. Exquisitely engraved on the wall, atop the throne was the Royal insignia. But sitting on its red velvet cushion was none other than the Shadow King.

'Bend your knee and bow to your King!' he rasped.

Luis refused, and calmly put his right hand on his blade handle.

'How dare you enter my castle, and defy a royal order!'

'This isn't your castle,' said Luis confidently.

'This castle and Adastra have been under my dominion for months. Surely you've seen my dark decorations across the land?'

'What you've done is horrible. What kind of King absorbs his own people?'

The Shadow King rose from his throne.

'A King that wants more power...that sensation you get when you realize you have power over someone else is something we all yearn. Once you get it you can in-still fear in others, and it's always better to be feared then loved. No one in life wants less power. We all want more…'

Luis looked disgusted.

'I remember when I first sprung forth into this world, a wish made by the former King. You see,
residing in everyone including yourself, deep within the crevices of your heart, exists a dark entity, where hatred, fear, and jealousy reside. The dark parts of the soul that we're told to regress...I'm just the little dark voice in everyone's mind personified.'

'The King had just lost his children in an accident.
It's natural to have such thoughts when going through adversity,' said Luis.

'Nonsense! Thoughts like that fill me with rage.
Adastra is full of fools with stupid banal thoughts.

Which is why I came and took over. There was no need for a coronation. I crowned myself, and I covered the land in darkness. Such silly people looking up to the moon and stars for guidance. I gave them all a harsh taste of reality...I covered the stars to remove their hope, I cursed the moon to kidnap their faith, and I stole their shadows to destroy their power. I made everyone, equal. Months went by and the people became recluses. Keeping things to themselves whilst I prospered - a land fit for a King! Then one day, through some lunar intervention, you arrived on this land. And together with the fisherman's daughter you set out on this pathetic fetch quest to retrieve the moon medals. I must admit, the two of you surprised me. I didn't think anyone knew of their ancient power.

Which is why I placed three of my knights to guard each one, and you defeated them all...and now I suppose you plan on dealing me a similar fate?'

Luis, not being intimidated by his glare, continued to stare at him.

'Little do you know I placed them there at the start of my reign, out of fear! But so much time has passed, since then I've been through a dark chrysalis, growing stronger every minute.'

The Shadow King materialized his sword-axe and held it high in the air.

'As of now, you and the girl are the only two that

remain in the whole of Adastra. That leaves a substantial amount of pressure on your shoulders. Aren't you worried child?'

'Worry gives a small thing a big shadow,' said Luis.

The Shadow King laughed at his words, and walked down the small steps.

'I'm going to give you one last chance to leave my castle. If you do…you and the girl will rest in peace, but if you choose to stay...then the sound of your screams will shun the light, and crack the moon once more!'

Luis took a deep breath in. He could feel his fear conjuring inside his mind. He stared at the King with intense focus and tightened the grip on his blade handle.

'Such misguided valor and gallantry! So be it, Adastra and its dark skies and murky waters will be your burial ground!'

The Shadow King walked toward Luis, his spiked armor clanked together, and he held his deathly sword-axe high in the air. The small voice in Luis's head screamed "Retreat!" but he chose not to listen. Instead he unsheathed the Luna blade. The sound of steel scraped the scabbard and the harsh white light surprised the Shadow King. Luis charged toward him and struck at him with the blade. The King defended his blows and retreated back. Luis continued to strike him, the bite of his blade stronger with the light. The

Shadow King fell on the steps near the throne, Luis swung at him and his spiked shoulder panels broke off. He raised the sword to deliver a final blow, but the King evaporated into the darkness! Luis looked around everywhere, and the King's laughter filled the room.

'Don't become so confident child, remember who you are fighting!'

Suddenly the room filled with a black vapor. Luis moved around in circles, trying to anticipate the King's movements, but unexpectedly the King appeared behind him and slashed his sword. Luis dodged at the last moment but a small gash appeared on his shoulder. Luis wiped away the blood with his finger and ran to the corner of the room. He can't creep up behind me now, he thought. He was wrong. Suddenly the King materialized in front of him and hacked at him. Luis jumped out of the way and ran toward the throne. Once again the King appeared, this time kicking Luis with his boot, who rolled down the steps and crashed onto the cold marble floor. Luis looked around, he couldn't let this carry on. He had to find a way to get rid of the mist, and clear his vision. Holding the Luna blade up in the air, he spun it around as fast as he could, the light acting as vacuum sucked in all of the dark cloud. The room and his vision became clear again, and the King, with no place to hide reappeared. Luis ran toward him and engaged another sword duel.

Luis aimed his blows at the Kings heart - each hit delivering huge damage to his armor. Luis dodged the King's responses with speed and accuracy, and battled back with calculated strikes that stung with light. Finally, the square panel protecting the Kings heart fell off. Luis raised his sword, but all of a sudden the King knelt down on one knee and lowered his head.

'Please don't...I admit defeat,' he gasped.

Luis stopped his swing and stood there holding his blade.

'Leave Adastra for good and take your darkness with you,' said Luis confidently.

The King raised his hand slowly, and dematerialized his sword-axe.

'As you wish.'

All of the dark fog encompassing the castle roof vanished. Luis turned to his right, opened the balcony doors, and stared at the horizon. The fog around the castle had cleared but when he looked up to the sky he realized the dark clouds were still covering the stars. In an instant, his face changed from wonder to regret. But it was too late. The Shadow King sprung up, and smacked Luis with his spiked helmet. Luis dropped the blade, and the King grabbed his throat with his left hand and raised him up in the air. Luis watched as the Kings right arm manifested into a horrifying black spike. In one swift move he swung his arm, and pierced

Luis's abdomen, injecting him with
a black venom.

'Foolish child, you should never let your guard down so easily.'

Luis looked at his wrist's veins turning black with each passing second.   He kicked his legs in the air, but nothing would break the Shadow King's evil grip.

'The second this toxin reaches your heart, you'll disappear into the darkness, just like your stupid friend Mr Plato.'

Luis shut his eyes and remembered Plato's final words.

'That's it give in to your fears, let the darkness take you!'

The wind from outside blew through his hair and suddenly he thought of something. Luis concentrated hard and raised his right hand. A huge gust of wind blasted into the room and lifted the blade back into his hands. Luis, in perfect striking distance, plunged the Luna blade deep into the King's heart of darkness. He let out a terrifying roar and a huge wave of light emanated from his body. Luis dropped to the floor and the dark toxin pouring through his veins ceased. The Shadow King evaporated, and the royal armor fell to the ground. Luis sat up and checked his wounds. But they were gone. He turned to the right, and looked out the window and watched as the dark cloud barrier vanished, and the stars in the sky slowly emerged.

Hearing the sound of footsteps he looked over to the door and spotted Marina.

She ran over to him, and picked him up.

'Luis are you alright?'

'It's done,' he gasped.

'You mean it's over...the Shadow Kings gone?'

Luis pointed to the ground, and she spotted the royal armor on the floor. Marina hugged and squeezed him tight, and he shut his tired eyes. But when he opened his eyes, he spotted a small silhouetted figure near the door. In shock he released himself immediately.

'Marina, who's that!?'

'Look who I found on the cliff,' she said.

The figure moved into the light, and it turned out to be Mr Plato. Luis smiled - he was happy to see him.

'Luis you actually did it! I knew you had it in you! How can I repay you for saving my life?' asked Plato.

'If it wasn't for your advice about the Luna cape and blade, I wouldn't have been able to save you, so consider us even, said Luis with a smile.'

Mr Plato, with a concerned look on his face, looked down the hall.

'What is it?' asked Luis.

'Luis I want to show you something...will you follow me?'

'Yeah, sure.' He turned to Marina who was admiring

the view from the balcony.

'Marina, you coming? Mr Plato has something he wants us to see.'

'Yeah, just give me five minutes,'

Luis looked at her and felt a warm feeling inside. He was glad to see her truly happy. Mr Plato called Luis again, who followed him out of the throne room, and took him to a door in one of the hallways.

'Luis this is the King's bedroom...'

Luis looked at him in astonishment.

'Now that the Shadow King is gone, you can finally meet the real King of Adastra.'

Mr Plato tried to open the door handle, but it wouldn't budge.

'That's strange...why won't it open?' said Mr Plato.

He barged on the door, and tried again, but it still wouldn't open.

'It doesn't make sense. When The Shadow King was reigning over Adastra, there was a weird dark seal covering the door. But you vanquished him, so why isn't the door opening?'

Luis confounded, stared at the door. There was a open window nearby, and he could hear the sound of the ocean crashing into the rocks. He walked over slowly and looked out. The full moon was shining, and the stars were out. As he stared at the dark ocean, Marina's words when she was first describing Adastra, flashed into his mind.

"The sea...used to shine an elegant emerald green"

A cold chill took over his body and he ran back down the hallway as fast as he could. Back in the throne room, Marina was gone. He looked everywhere for her but couldn't find her. In the corner of his eye he seen something moving on the balcony. He rushed out and saw Marina standing on the edge. There was a shadowy figure with crimson eyes and black tentacle like arms standing next to her. One of its arms was wrapped around her neck.

'She loves the ocean so much, I doubt she'll mind if she's buried in it.' rasped the Shadow King.

Marina screamed for Luis's help, and he slowly moved his hand to the Luna blade.

'Don't be so stupid! Draw your weapon and I drop her!'

Luis put his hand in the air, and apologized to Marina.

'Here's your last lesson, one that will be marked with her death. It's not how you start, but how you finish!' scathed the Shadow King.

Marina peered over the edge - hundreds of feet below the ocean waves were smashing into the rocks. She started shaking, looked at Luis one last time, and closed her eyes. In one quick instant, Luis drew the Luna blade and using the wind's power accelerated toward her. He swiped at Shadow Kings arm - breaking his grip on Marina. Luis still holding on to him, flew off into the night sky, reaching break-neck speed! Luis flung his gaseous body in front of the full moon. He rocketed toward him and slayed the Shadow King directly under the moonlight. Banishing him from Adastra, once and for all.

CHAPTER SEVEN

Promise The Moon

"Shoot for the moon, even if you miss you'll land among the stars"

- Les Brown

Under the light of the moon the Shadow King shattered into thousands of pieces. Luis hovering in the sky, watched as the small black particles from his body disintegrated and vaporized. Many feet below, the Sea of Serenity's somber surface transitioned back to its illustrious emerald green. Luis swooped back onto the castle balcony and picked up Marina.

'It's finally over,' he said in a calm and confident voice.
'Thank you for saving me.'

Luis hugged her tight, she shut her eyes, and rested her head on his shoulders. Mr Plato joined them on the balcony.

'Luis, Marina, are you okay?'

Luis looked at him tiredly.

'We're fine,' said Luis.

'I saw everything. Well done,' said Mr Plato.

'How can we be sure he won't come back?' asked Luis.
'That evil Shadow is gone...you destroyed him in front
of the moon, and the light suffused his soul...it won't
return I assure you.'
Luis let go of Marina, and they both turned to him.
'Now that he's gone for good...Luis, Marina, there's
someone I'd like you to meet.'
Marina looked at Luis in confusion, but he knew whom
Mr Plato was speaking of.
Back in the castle hallway, the trio stood outside a
wooden door. Mr Plato put his hand on the door
handle, and pushed it down. Marina looked at Luis,
who was just as nervous as she was. They had
overcome so many obstacles, travelled far and wide,
and now they were finally going to meet the King of
Adastra. Mr Plato opened the door and they all
stepped inside the King's bedroom. The velvet curtains
were drawn, and it was hauntingly dark. Mr Plato
opened them immediately and the starlight poured into
the room. The walls were an angelic white, and
hanging down above the stone fireplace was a family
portrait in a gold frame. The carpet was plush red and
there was a small spiraling staircase leading up to the
castle roof. Luis and Marina stood near a four poster
bed, its sheer drapes were closed, and a faint sound of
breathing could be heard. Marina tightly held Luis's
arm in anticipation as Mr Plato pulled back the drapes.

Lying down on the bed was an old man with white hair and a white beard. The light from outside broke through the filter of the curtains and lit the side of his face. He was very pale, and there were heavy, dark bruised bags under his eyes. Mr Plato lifted the man's veiny hands, which seemed cold and he quickly turned on the automatic fireplace. A subtle warmth filled the room, and even though the old man wanted to speak, he couldn't. Luis watched him move his purple chapped lips up and down, and tried to decipher his words. Suddenly the old man let out a huge wheezing cough, and opened his eyes. Mr Plato finally smiled.

'Luis, Marina, meet your majesty - King Jorge of Adastra.'

Luis and Marina didn't know what to do, Marina took a chance and curtseyed, and Luis simply bowed.

A smile appeared on the Kings wrinkled face.

'It's good to see you again sire,' said Mr Plato.

The King coughed, and rubbed his eyes.

'How are you feeling?' asked Marina curiously.

'Where are my manners?' Mr Plato cleared his throat.

'Your majesty, this is Marina, and the boy next to her, Luis. They have travelled all the way here to come visit you.'

'I know who they are Plato,' said the King calmly.

Mr Plato looked at him surprised.

'From the moment they set off from Oasis Island, I've

been with them in spirit. Watching from my dreams.'

As Luis and Marina looked on in awe, The King cleared his throat, and spoke again.

'Before I say thank you, I must apologize for my erratic behavior over the past months. I certainly have not acted like a King. All of these events have transpired because of my selfish behavior. I'm sure Plato has told you both what happened?'

Luis and Marina nodded their heads.

'Never become so enslaved by your own selfish and hatred demands, that you become possessed. Look at me...my body and my mind has slowly atrophied. You must promise me, you'll never let that happen.'

He started couching again, and Mr Plato re-arranged his pillows, allowing him to sit up straight.

'In my deep slumber I have been following your journey. It started out as nightmare, and now it's ended up a peaceful dream. You two have shown such daring determination, and candor in expression, and from all that's left of me, I thank you.'

'We have something to show you sir,' said Luis.

'For all your troubles Luis, please call me Jorge,' said the King and he smiled at him.

'What is it you wish to show me?'

Luis pulled out Mr Plato's diary entry from his back pocket, and showed it to the King. He took it, and Luis watched his pensive eyes scan the page. Mr Plato not expecting this, looked on extremely nervous.

'King Jorge, this was Mr Plato's diary entry on the day of the accident,' said Luis.

'He really did care a lot for your children,' added Marina.

The King finished reading it, folded it in half, and handed it back to Luis.

'Plato, I am sorry for the way I treated you. I was hurt as you can imagine, and I'll admit I was a little jealous.'

'Jealous? What do you mean?' asked Mr Plato.

'I was always so busy with my royal errands, I never really got to spend time with my own children. You were always playing with them, and taking them out on fun trips. They would talk about you all the time, and sometimes, well I used to wonder if they loved you more.'

'Sir, I can assure you that's not true,' said Mr Plato.

'The prince and princess loved you both,' interrupted Luis.

The King and Mr Plato looked at Luis strangely, wanting an explanation of some sort.

'We met your children sir...the prince and princess,' said Marina.

Mr Plato looked stunned, and the King sat up.

'How is that possible?' he asked.

'On the way back from Mount Moon Cove, the Shadow King filled Adastra with darkness. We got stuck in the white water maze, but your children's spirits appeared and they navigated us to safety,' said Luis.

The King and Mr Plato hung on Luis's every word.

'They had a message for you...they wanted us to tell you, to stop grieving, and to not be so upset. They wanted you to know that they're happy in the afterlife.'

Marina looked up at Mr Plato.

'The prince said to tell you he misses you...'

She turned to the King.

'And to tell you that he loves you dearly.'

'Your children saved our lives,' added Luis.

Mr Plato and the King looked at each other reminiscently.

'We promised the prince we'd get the message to you, and now that we've defeated the Shadow King and returned Adastra to the way it was, they can finally rest in peace,' said Luis.

After a brief silence, the King began to cough uncontrollably. He looked at everyone longingly, and cleared his throat.

'There is something I need to tell you.'

The three of them leaned in curiously.

'I'm abdicating my throne.'

'Your majesty, you can't...your still in a state of convalescence, it's the illness talking!' yelled Mr Plato.

'No, it's not Plato, I assure you…I must go and be with

my children.'

'Be with your children?' asked Marina.

'You must look beyond the surface of my words...I'm abdicating the throne, as well as my spirit.'

'But your majesty, if you leave, who will rule over Adastra?' asked Mr Plato.

'Adastra is full of wonderful people, it will find another worthy ruler. I am in no position to be a King. My mind has weakened, and my body has broken down. With each painful cough, I can already feel myself slipping away...over the past months I've been in a mental prison. If I try to rule again, those dark feelings may come to the surface, and that's a risk I'm not willing to take. The only way for me to release myself, is to go and be with the two people I love most...my children. That's the only way I'll have perpetual freedom.'

Mr Plato looked on, and it dawned on him that the King couldn't carry on.

'I'm going to miss you Jorge,' said Mr Plato.

'You have always been my best friend Plato, I want you to know that.'

The King looked at Luis and Marina.

'If it wasn't for the two of you, Adastra would be covered in darkness. You have a great spirit of adventure, a trait which is seldom seen in these times. Most people like to play in shallow water, only getting their feet wet. You have proven if you dive deep into the ocean, not only do you experience new things, but the water takes a different hue. You find the iridescent coral, and you encounter different creatures. But more importantly you find yourselves not wanting to return to the surface. You must promise yourselves that you'll always keep going further, pushing your boundaries and expanding your horizons.'

The King outstretched his hand to Marina and she shook it, squeezing it tightly.

'The beautiful fisherman's daughter, with wisdom beyond her young years. Thank you.'

Finally he turned his attention to Luis, and shook his hand.

'Words cannot express how thankful I am for your endeavors. To come to a land you're not familiar with and acclimate yourself so quickly, takes a vast amount of belief and courage. And without those traits, you cannot practice anything in life consistently. Not only have you returned the tide to Adastra, you've become the tide that rises the boats around them.'

He looked up at the three smiling faces around his bed.

'Thank you, all of you…farewell and take good care of Adastra.'

The King smiled, closed his eyes, and laid down to rest perpetually.

*

After a nostalgic silence Marina walked to the fireplace. She took Mr Plato's diary entry and threw it into the flames.

'This will be our secret Mr Plato, if the people of Adastra find out what really happened, they might not take it so well.'

'Thank you for believing in my story, and going to such lengths to prove my innocence,' said Mr Plato.

The trio watched as the paper burned to ash in the ember.

Mr Plato noticed Luis was awfully silent.

'Luis I'm sure you're wondering how to return home?'

He looked at Mr Plato and smiled to himself.

'Come to think of it, I haven't thought about it for a while, but yes I'd like to know.'

'It is simple. You must go to a point in the water where the two worlds collide. Perhaps a spot where the moon is reflecting on the water's surface. Think of a suitable place you know, and jump.'

Luis started to remember how he landed in Adastra and now it all started to make sense. Luis hugged and thanked him, but Marina broke their peaceful moment.

'Wow! I can't believe it!' yelled Marina who was looking out the King's bedroom window. She ran up the stairs and went through the door, leading to the castle roof.

'Luis you have to see this! Come quick!'

'You better go after her, I think she has something incredible to show you,' said Mr Plato.

Luis followed her up on to the castle roof, and stared in astonishment at the beautiful blue moon. The Sea of Serenity's surface reflected the myriad of stars, adorning the velvety texture of the night sky.

'Wow it's amazing,' said Luis softly.

He took Marina's hand and walked to the very edge of the rooftop. Marina slightly frightened shut her eyes.

'Being on the edge isn't safe, but the view is better,' whispered Luis.

He held her tight...

'Marina, open your eyes.'

She gasped at the spectacular view, and they gazed at the stars longingly.

'Luis, I just realized, it's going to take us forever to return to Oasis Island.'

He looked at her and smiled.

'That's because you think we're going back by boat,' said Luis.

'Well how else are we getting back?'

Luis took her hand and turned to the wind.

'Don't let go,' he said calmly.

A warm breeze tore through the air, and using the power of the Luna cape, Luis lifted them both up. Holding Marina from her slender waist, he shot forward and flew toward the blue moon. Gliding in the gale they flew through some wispy clouds, and past the shooting stars. The cape whipped in the wind, and Luis soared past Emerald Bay Island. All of its inhabitants were out and about, and they looked up in awe as Luis and Marina rocketed past. He darted right and flew through Sparkling Coral's beauteous light show. Down below in the water a small blue spark flashed up like a flare, and the pair waved at Núria some feet below. Luis accelerated towards Aquatic Reef, and swooped through the forestation, leaves fell off the trees as he flew past, and a chorus of chitters from the animals rang through their ears. He spotted Oasis Island in the distance and increased his speed. Marina's eyes squinted with the force of the wind.

'Hold on tight,' said Luis calmly.

He swerved downward at an exhilarating speed, and descended onto the boardwalk. It rattled with the force, and Luis let go of Marina. She turned to him, and brushed her hair away from her face.

'That was amazing! Thank you!'

'Well, you always said, you wanted me to see the real Adastra, and now I have.'

They walked back through the beach and toward her house.

'Home sweet home,' said Marina.

She knocked on the door, and after a long pause, it

finally swung open. Luis and Marina looked up shocked.

'Raul!' shouted Marina.

She jumped up onto him and squeezed him tight.

'How did you get here?' asked Marina.

'Uncle Bruno sailed over here a couple of hours ago when I was still unconscious. But about an hour ago I woke up, and now I feel great!'

He looked over at Luis who was standing by the door.

'It's good to see you again Raul,' said Luis.

'Well I have you to thank for that,' said Raul as he shook Luis's hand.

'You look like you've been through a hell of a lot.'

'I have...we both have, but it's finally over,' said Luis.

A loud voice rattled through the doorway

'What's all that noise out there!?' yelled Marina's mother.

She walked into the hall and spotted the trio at the door.

'Marina! Luis!'

She yelled for Marina's father and Uncle Bruno and they scurried quickly to the door.

'Where have you two been? You've had me worried sick!' yelled Marina's mother.

Luis and Marina looked up at all of them standing there, and in unison they started laughing.

*

The fireplace warmed the room and all of the family sat on the edge of their seats as Luis and Marina told them of their amazing journey. They drank soup, rested for a short while, and after a few hours Luis got up and flashed a sad look at them.

'I think it's time I said goodbye.'

He unclipped the Luna Blade and handed it to Marina's Uncle.

'This belongs to you Bruno. Thank you for instilling in me the heart and mind of a warrior.'

'My pleasure,' said Bruno calmly.

Luis took off the Luna Cape, stared at it, and smiled.

He handed it to Marina's father.

'I believe this belongs to you.'

Marina's father held it up and looked at it in awe.

'I always knew there was something special about it, I'm glad you put it to good use!'

Luis downed his soup and turned to Marina's mother.

'Thank you so much for your hospitality.'

Lastly, he turned to Raul.

'Thank you for teaching me how to apply the hidden lessons that can be learnt from failure. When I first met you I looked up to you so much, and I'm glad to see you back on your feet.'

'You really have changed Luis...thank you for saving my life,' said Raul.

Marina got up and walked toward the door.

'I'm gonna walk Luis to the boardwalk.'

Luis thanked them all one last time, and walked to the end of the boardwalk with Marina.

She looked over toward the rocks where she first spotted Luis washed up on the shore.

'It's amazing isn't it, how much we achieved just by following one small idea.'

Luis looked at the spot and reflected on her words.

'Marina do you remember when we were sailing and you told me how everything happens for a reason? At first I was superstitious, but now I think you're right. Those dark clouds that were barricading the stars, I think they were there for a reason...not to stop us from seeing them, but for making us earn the right to see them. If we instantly got everything we wished for, we'd never grow...I think it just proves if you follow what you love, and you endure the hardships along the way, then you deserve to see the stars, and in time you will.'

'I'm glad we did,' said Marina.

All of a sudden he spotted something moving on the boardwalk floor.

'Hey Marina look! Your shadows come back...so has mine!'

She spun round in a circle to make sure it was really there.

'Wow I didn't even notice it! I guess I just got used to not seeing it.'

Marina's family were outside the house watching from the distance. Luis looked up at the blue moon, and glanced at its reflection glistening on the on the Sea of Serenity's surface.

'Mr Plato said to draw upon my memory of a suitable place I know, and jump.'

Luis started to think, but Marina abruptly de-railed his train of thought.

'I'm going to miss you so much Luis...please don't go...stay here in Adastra.'

Luis looked at her longingly.

'I'd love to stay in Adastra with you Marina, but I can't. I'm going to miss this place too, but I have to return home...'

He walked over to her and stared into her hazel eyes.

'I must follow on with my original mission.'

'I understand...I'm sorry Luis. Follow your heroic heart, and no matter what happens on your journey, be persistent and everlasting, like the waves lapping the shore.'

Luis hugged her and kissed her on the cheek.

'I'm gonna miss you Marina. Thank you for your words of wisdom, I couldn't have saved Adastra without you...from now on, whenever I look up at the crescent moon, I'm going to remember your smile.'

Luis gently let go, and walked toward the edge of the boardwalk.

'There will always be a place in the sky for your star,' said Marina.

Luis looked back and smiled at her one last time.

'Goodbye Marina.'

He leapt high into the air and dived into the moon's reflection, leaving Adastra for good.

*

Luis opened his eyes and resurfaced from the pool on the cruise ship. It was still late and no one was around. He climbed out of the pool and started to breathe heavily. His wet clothes weighed him down, and he leaned over the deck railing to get his breath back. He looked around in awe wondering if the whole thing was a dream. His heart was beating rapidly and he put his hand over it to check. By surprise he pulled out the Moon Medallion – he'd forgotten to give it back. He smiled to himself and walked toward the ship's bow.

There was a magnificent blue moon illuminating the night sky, and he knew the whole experience had been real. In the aquatic ambience, he looked up toward the stars shining in the vista.

'Goodnight moon, we'll meet one day in person...

I promise.'

THE END

ACKNOWLEDGMENTS

First and foremost I would like to thank my good friends Milo and Nilan. Their support over the years has been instrumental in helping me helping me follow my dreams, and aiding me in my quest of bringing stories to life.

Secondly I'd like to thank Paul for his assistance throughout the long writing process. His words of wisdom have deftly guided me past pitfalls, and his support has been immeasurable, I am eternally grateful.

I would like to thank my close friend Victor, for his continued enthusiasm for my work and this project. Congratulations on your new role as a proud father, I hope one day your son reads this book, and shares it with his friends.

I would also like to thank Gilbert for believing in me over the years. He really is the embodiment of someone who lives, loves, and laughs.

I'd like to thank Nimi, the hardest working person I've ever met. If anyone should collide with perpetual success it should be him.

I would also like to thank Mr Alexander, my high school English teacher. He never constricted my creativity, and he made writing a joy.

Many thanks to Hans and Jonathan, for teaching me the power of curiosity, the spirit of adventure, and for showing me a whole new reality.

Thanks to Brent for instilling in me the power of indifference, and teaching me how to reframe situations to take my life to the next level.

Finally, I would like to thank all the beautiful, feminine women I've met - that have inspired me throughout my journey. You are the anima, the spirit, and the soul of my work - those reading this you know who you are. This book is for you...

- Joaquim Silva

The Story Continues...

facebook.com/BeyondTheLuna

twitter - @Joaquim_Silva_

#BeyondTheLuna

Per aspera ad astra
Through hardships to the stars

Printed in Great Britain
by Amazon.co.uk, Ltd.,
Marston Gate.